The Black Stallion's Sulky Colt

The Black Stallion's second son, Bonfire, was a problem colt. A track accident had turned him into a frightened, rebellious horse who couldn't be relied upon in a race.

When Alec Ramsay and his old friend Henry Dailey took over his training, time was running out. Only two weeks remained before the top event of the harness-racing season, the grueling Hambletonian. Bonfire had a chance to win—if he could lose the terrible fear that haunted him.

Books by
WALTER FARLEY

The Black Stallion
The Black Stallion Returns
Son of the Black Stallion
The Island Stallion
The Black Stallion and Satan
The Black Stallion's Blood Bay Colt
The Island Stallion's Fury
The Black Stallion's Filly
The Black Stallion Revolts
The Black Stallion's Sulky Colt
The Island Stallion Races
The Black Stallion's Courage
The Black Stallion Mystery
The Black Stallion and Flame
The Black Stallion Challenged!
The Black Stallion's Ghost
The Black Stallion and the Girl
The Horse-Tamer
Man o' War

*All titles available in both paperback
and hardcover editions*

The Black Stallion's
Sulky Colt

by WALTER FARLEY

RANDOM HOUSE  NEW YORK

Library of Congress Cataloging in Publication Data

Farley, Walter
The black stallion's sulky colt
New York, Random House [1954]
I. Title   PZ10.3.F22.Bms   54-7011 [68q½]
ISBN: 0-394-80610-7 (trade hardcover)
        0-394-90610-1 (library binding)
        0-394-83917-X (trade hardcover)

For Frank Chesbro and Bi Shively—
and for the real Bonfire and Stanley Dancer,
who started out together

Contents

Night Race

1

Alec Ramsay was on the train that had left New York City's Pennsylvania Station at 7:05 P.M. and would arrive at Roosevelt Raceway, Westbury, Long Island, by eight o'clock. This would be a half-hour before the first race of the evening, giving him time to locate Bonfire, the second son of the Black Stallion.

He wondered about this three-year-old colt, whom he had never seen. Had the Black stamped Bonfire as his own in body, head and temperament? Or had that small, quiet harness-racing mare been the more dominant in marking her son? Soon he'd know, and he looked forward eagerly to meeting Bonfire and watching him race beneath the lights in a sport Alec had known previously only at county and state fairs.

He turned away from the window, where the suburban apartment buildings were giving way to more and more areas of spacious green. He was thankful he wore only a light sport shirt, for the July day had been extremely hot and the coming night promised little relief.

The car was crowded, with every seat taken and men standing in the aisles. The stranger sitting beside him was absorbed in reading a long typewritten statement, but suddenly he looked up, caught Alec's eyes, and said, "Sometimes I think a trainer does a better job of training the owner than he does the horse."

Alec glanced at the paper, this time noting the letterhead which read, "FRED RINGO'S STABLE." Quietly he said, "That all depends on the trainer and the owner."

"Take this item," the stranger went on. "Leg lotion, two dollars and fifty cents. My wife claims my colt uses more lotion than she does. And I can't even tell her what it's for."

Alec smiled. "Leg lotion is a mild liniment they put on a horse's legs before doing him up," he said.

The man looked at Alec. "You mean you know something about horses?"

"A little."

"Then maybe you can explain a few of these other items I'm paying for. My wife says it's time I found out. But it's hard to pin Freddy Ringo down, especially on race night. What's this *foot* grease?" He grinned. "Make him go faster?"

"Not directly," Alec answered. "Although anything you do to keep a horse's feet in good condition is bound to help his speed. Foot grease is put on hoofs to keep them soft and to prevent cracks."

"How about this clay for packing feet?" the man asked, turning to his statement again.

"Pounding a hard racetrack day after day often results in a horse's feet becoming hot and wet. The clay is used overnight to help draw out the heat."

"You seem to know more than just a *little* about this game," the man said. "Do you own a harness racer too?"

"No."

The man put out his right hand. "My name is Dick Frecon," he said. "I own the three-year-old colt Lively Man. Guess you've seen him out here."

Alec shook the man's hand. "No, I haven't been here before. My name is Ramsay . . . Alec Ramsay."

Frecon's heavy eyebrows bunched quickly. "What did you say your name was?" he asked. His gaze had left Alec's face, wandering to the boy's large hands, then to the broad shoulders.

"Ramsay," Alec repeated.

Frecon was studying his face. "Not the *jockey*," he said. "Not the one who was up on the Black and Satan . . . and last year, Black Minx. Not *that* Alec Ramsay."

"They're our horses," Alec admitted.

"Well, what do you know!" Frecon said incredulously. "For years I've been following you and never getting closer than the nearest grandstand." He folded his statement and put it away. "And now that I've switched sports I find myself sitting next to you, *even asking if you know horses*!" Patting his pocket, he said, "Sorry about all those questions."

"You needn't be," Alec said. "If anyone has a horse in training he should know what he's paying for."

"That's what my wife says." For a moment they rode in silence, then Frecon said, "Do you mind my asking what you're doing out here?"

"There's a colt I want to see," Alec said. "He's going in the second race."

"Why, that's my colt's race too!" Frecon said, sitting up

straighter in his seat. "What do you have in it?"

"I don't have anything in it," Alec said, smiling. "But the colt's name is Bonfire. He's sired by the Black."

"Oh, sure, I should have thought of that since the boys were talking about him last week. Seems he was a whirlwind last year at two, but he hasn't done much this season. He's owned by a Jimmy Creech of Coronet, Pennsylvania."

"That's right," Alec said. "Mr. Creech is an old friend of my partner, Henry Dailey. That's how his harness mare happened to be bred to the Black."

"I'd sure like to meet Henry Dailey," Frecon said, "—and the Black and Satan."

"Then why don't you come up to the farm sometime? We're only a two-hour ride from New York."

"I sure will. I'd love to, if you're sure it's all right."

"Of course it's all right," Alec said.

The train was slowing, coming into the station at Westbury.

"I can't wish this Bonfire much luck tonight," Frecon said, "not with my colt in the same race. Who's driving him anyway? One of the big trainers?"

"No, he's being trained and driven by a young fellow named Tom Messenger. I don't know anything about him except that he comes from Coronet and is a friend of Mr. Creech, who's sick at home and can't be here."

"Then you know this Jimmy Creech?"

"No, I don't know him, either." Alec smiled. "I don't know anyone," he added, ". . . not even Bonfire. I'm just looking forward to meeting them."

"Well," Frecon said, standing up as the train stopped, "I can't say I mind hearing about this Tom Messenger driving

Bonfire. I wouldn't like to see a son of the Black in the hands of any of the top men out here. Not with my colt in the same race and with hay at seventy dollars a ton!"

Later Alec moved with the crowd streaming through the main entrance gate of Roosevelt Raceway. It was not yet dark but the track lights were already on. Dance music came over the public-address system.

Approaching the track, he saw the large paddock to his right and turned toward it. A policeman stopped him at the gate.

"I want to see Tom Messenger," Alec said.

"Are you an owner?"

"Yes."

That was true. And after all, thought Alec, the policeman hadn't asked him what horse he owned or if the horse was here.

Alec entered the paddock area where he found all the horses stabled for the evening's program. He went down the row marked "2nd Race," for Bonfire had post position eight in the second race. When he came to the eighth stall he saw that the boy in racing silks and the old groom beside him were busy, so he just stood quietly and looked at the colt.

Bonfire was cross-tied. He was a beautiful colt with fine racy lines and startling color. It was easy to see where he had got his name, for his coat was as red as fire, in striking contrast to the heavy black mane and tail. Alec noted the colt's small, sensitive head and the nostrils that kept moving constantly. Bonfire was hot and blowing.

The bald-headed groom squeezed a sponge over Bonfire's head, and the colt sought to catch the downward streams with his tongue. Alec ventured a friendly "Hello" but the man went on with his job as though he hadn't heard.

Alec studied the rest of Bonfire, noting the long legs, chest and hindquarters which, like the head, had been inherited from the Black. But there was no doubt that Bonfire had got his neck from his dam. It was shorter and more muscular than his sire's. Alec remembered Volo Queen well. He had taken care of her during the three months she had been at the farm.

Bonfire's rapidly moving eyes were on him. Alec raised a hand to pat the wet forehead but suddenly the groom's smooth, hairless skull was between him and the colt.

"What do you want?" The old man shifted a plug of tobacco from one side of his mouth to the other. "I asked you that before."

"Sorry," Alec said. "I didn't hear you. I was looking at your colt."

"I know that. Step back now. I can't work with you in my way."

Alec stepped out of the stall.

"What'd you say you wanted?" the old man asked again. Before Alec could answer, the man moved to the side of the colt and spoke to the boy wearing racing silks. "What do you think, Tom? Did he hit his knee going that last trip?"

The boy bent low beside Bonfire's left foreleg. "No, George, but I was worried he had," he said in a husky voice. As he stood up, the loose red-and-white racing jacket made his tall, gaunt body look heavier than it was. He turned to Alec questioningly.

"I'm Alec Ramsay. I own the Black," Alec explained. "I

wanted to meet you and see this colt."

"Oh," the boy said, "I've read a lot about you. George," turning to the old man, "this fellow owns Bonfire's sire. He's a race-rider."

"That ain't racin'," George said disinterestedly. "You got to sit behind 'em to race. Get the sheet on him now, Tom."

Alec smiled and rubbed the colt's head. His name meant nothing to George. Neither did the Black, except as the sire of Bonfire. The old man was far removed from the world in which Alec and the Black lived and raced. "Jimmy Creech wrote to look you up," he said.

George and Tom stopped working then.

"He did? Why?" Tom Messenger asked, concern in his eyes.

"Nothing special," Alec assured him. "My partner at the farm, Henry Dailey, got a letter from him. Jimmy just mentioned that you were at Roosevelt Raceway and to look you up. I guess he figured we'd be interested in seeing Bonfire race."

Seemingly relieved, George and Tom went on with their work.

Alec didn't mind their abruptness. After all, he had come only to see this colt by the Black. Yet he would have liked to have asked them why Bonfire had been worked so short a time before his race. Perhaps later they'd tell him. He turned away from Bonfire and looked over the other horses in the second race. They too were breathing heavily and were covered.

George came out of the stall. "Tom, where'd I put those wire cutters I brought over from the barn? I want to fix that wheel spoke."

"In your pocket, George."

"Oh, yeah." George spat tobacco juice on the ground and took the wire cutters from his pocket.

Alec waited until George had fixed the sulky wheel. Then he said, "Don't you find that it hurts your horses to stand them in their stalls while they're hot?"

George entered the stall and pulled Bonfire's blanket up on his wet neck. "That's the way it's done," he said abruptly.

Tom, who was again down beside the colt's right foreleg, looked up, studying Alec for a second; then he too turned back to Bonfire.

Alec said nothing more, although such a practice was contrary to everything Henry had taught him. The rule was that you could not *stand* hot horses without doing harm to their muscles. Yet here they were doing just that.

Alec talked to Bonfire and the colt's ears pricked forward, almost touching at the tips. Occasionally George and Tom stopped their work to listen to Alec.

The sky was now dark but the great lights made Roosevelt Raceway as bright as day. The mammoth stands had filled and the crowd was waiting. Suddenly a bell in the paddock sounded, calling the horses in the first race to the post. At the end of the row Alec saw eight horses, pulling light racing sulkies, file onto the track. The drivers slid into their seats, taking up the long lines as grooms stepped away from their charges.

Alec, who had never before seen a harness race at a night track, would have liked to watch the race. But he was more interested in Bonfire, so he remained in the stall with George and Tom.

When the paddock judge came down the row, Alec

stepped closer to Bonfire. He knew he would be told to leave if he was asked for his paddock pass and couldn't produce one. Suddenly a cloth was placed in his hand.

George said, "Start workin' if you want to stay here. Get his legs."

Alec bent quickly and ran the cloth down Bonfire's forelegs. The official stopped outside the stall for a moment and then walked on.

"Thanks," Alec said. He couldn't see George, who was on the other side of the colt. "I *did* want to stay."

"Get his hind legs too," George ordered.

Tom Messenger watched but said nothing.

Alec felt a lot easier about being there. He'd been surprised by the unexpected assistance from George. Perhaps his mentioning Jimmy Creech was responsible for the old man's acceptance of his interest in Bonfire.

Alec heard the sound of a car's engine and the beat of many hoofs. The mobile starting gate was in motion and the horses were coming down the stretch for the beginning of the first race. The stands were still. Slowly the car's engine mounted to a high-pitched roar, silencing the hoofs behind it. Suddenly the noise of the engine died and only the rapid beat of hoofs and the cries of the drivers could be heard from the track. The stands came to life, a swelling sea of clamor, but above all else rose the voice of the announcer as he called the positions of the horses rounding the first turn.

Tom went to the front of the stall and looked out in the direction of the stands and the track. His long, thin face was very grave for one so young, Alec noticed. And his eyes held a troubled brightness.

George went up and stood beside Tom. "Why'n't you take

an aspirin?" he asked kindly.

"It wouldn't help me any now," Tom answered, turning away and going back to work on Bonfire.

George said, "Then stop thinking of this as more than what it is, just another race."

Alec couldn't see Tom but he heard him say almost in a whisper, "You know what Jimmy expects from us."

"I know what he expects all right," the old man answered. "But you and the colt can't do more'n your best. Like you been doin' at the fairs. This ain't no different except that it's night instead of day. Look at it that way an' you'll be all right."

"I just don't want to let Jimmy down, not now," the boy said in the same low voice.

"You won't, and the colt won't either," George answered.

Alec looked at the old man standing beside him. George's expression belied the confidence of his words. He was worried too.

The paddock judge moved down their row. "Hook 'em up, boys," he called. "You're next. Be ready to go in three minutes."

George led Bonfire from the stall and backed him between the shafts of the waiting sulky. He glanced at Alec in surprise as though he'd forgotten that he was there. Then he said, "You'd better look busy if you're stickin' around."

Working in silence, they drew the harness leather tight around the shafts. Tom took up the long lines. Finally George led Bonfire down the row while Tom and Alec walked beside the sulky.

Alec noticed that the strange brightness in Tom's eyes was greater than before. And his big hands were trembling, telegraphing his nervousness down the lines to his colt. This was the reason for Bonfire's tossing head and the wetness that was showing on his red body.

Alec understood Tom's nervousness, for often he had felt the same way before a race. Tom would be all right once he got into the sulky and the colt stepped onto the track. He'd calm down then and so would Bonfire.

The bugle call to the post came over the public-address system and the paddock gate was opened. The first horse stepped onto the track.

Tom slid into his seat behind the blood bay colt. "Okay, George," he said. "Let him go."

The old man stepped away from Bonfire's head. "Luck, Tom," he said.

"Thanks, George." Tom nodded as Alec too wished him good luck. He tried to grin but it didn't come off.

Alec followed George to the wooden bench just inside the track rail where other caretakers were sitting. From here he would be very close to Bonfire.

Alec said, "Don't worry about Tom. I'm sure he's okay now."

"I'm not so sure at all," the old man answered. "He's over-anxious. He's been that way all week. It's taken a lot out of him. He's apt to do 'most anything in this race."

Alec said nothing more for over the public-address system came the introductions.

"Ladies and gentlemen," the announcer said, "parading up the track now are the horses in the second race on your program. This is a stake race for three-year-olds who are eligible for the world-famed Hambletonian to be raced at Goshen, New York, on August seventh. This is an important preparatory race for that great classic, ladies and gentlemen, and from this field of fine colts may come the one who is destined to go down in harness-racing history as this year's winner of the Hambletonian. So watch them well.

"Number one is Lively Man, a roan colt by Titan Hanover out of Blue Maid. He is owned by Mr. Richard Frecon of New York City and is being driven by Fred Ringo. Number two is Silver Knight, a gray colt by Volomite out of Gray Dream. He is owned by Mr. Peter Conover of Venice, Florida, and is being driven by Ray O'Neil. Number three is Victory Boy, a brown colt . . ."

Alec watched the line of horses in parade, their glossy coats shining under the bright lights. All this was a far cry from the harness races he had seen at fairs. Here were no crowded midways with spinning Ferris wheels, no prize poultry and livestock to compete with the racehorse for the attention of the crowd. Here the racehorse alone was the attraction. A yellow crescent moon hung low in the night sky, while beneath it was the red glow of city lights. It was a beautiful setting for a race.

Alec turned around and looked back at the stands. Most of the people there had come from New York and adjacent suburban towns and cities. Probably few of them ever had the opportunity to see harness racing at the fairs. So it was at this raceway that they had become familiar with the sport and had learned to love it, making it what it was tonight.

The announcer had come to the last horse in the post parade. "Number eight is Bonfire, a blood bay colt by the Black out of Volo Queen. He is owned by Mr. Jimmy Creech of Coronet, Pennsylvania, and is being driven by Tom Messenger. Bonfire is making his first start at Roosevelt

Raceway since winning the Two-Year-Old Championship at this track last September."

Alec turned to George. "It's a short stretch to the turn. Does Bonfire get away fast?"

The old man kept his eyes on Bonfire and Tom. He didn't answer Alec.

The horses came down the track, taking their two warm-up scores before the start of the race. Bonfire's strides were low, even and effortless, his muscles standing out prominently beneath his wet, glossy coat. He paid no attention to the other colts. He was eager to be turned loose, his every movement disclosed it. Alec knew that Bonfire was a son worthy of the Black, and he watched him with great pride.

"What does he have to beat in this race?" he asked.

"All of 'em," George muttered.

Alec smiled. "I know, but any *one* in particular?"

"All of 'em," George repeated, his eyes never leaving the colts who were now going behind the long, open limousine at the far turn.

The announcer said, "The horses have reached the mobile gate and are now in the hands of the starter."

The barrier wings of the limousine stretched across the track. Alec could see the starter standing in the back of the car, talking through a microphone to the drivers and getting them into their post positions. Bonfire was on the far out-side and had his head close to the barrier. The car increased its speed coming down the stretch and the horses came along behind it. They neared the start. Suddenly the lights in the great stands dimmed. The car pulled away quickly to the outside of the track, its barrier wings folded. The brilliantly lighted track was the stage. The race was on!

Alec jumped to his feet as the horses came toward the first turn. George pulled him roughly down again so he could see. Bonfire was moving fast in an all-out drive. Alec heard Tom Messenger's voice raised above those of the other drivers, and he knew that Tom intended to get Bonfire out in front by the turn.

The moving line of surging horses and sulkies held; then there was a sudden merging of colored silks as the drivers bunched going into the turn. Tom had Bonfire out in front but not far enough to cut in safely in front of the others. Gleaming, silvery-spoked wheels spun crazily taking the heavy strain of the turn. Tom kept Bonfire on the outside as though determined to get far enough ahead to move safely over to the rail.

George's head was shaking miserably and he mumbled, "I knew it. I knew it. He's trying too hard. He'll knock the colt out."

Alec heard him but said nothing. All around the turn Tom kept Bonfire on the far outside, fighting for the lead. But for every two strides Bonfire took, the colts near the rail took only one without losing ground to him. Alec knew what racing on the outside meant to any horse, especially a young colt. Tom was sacrificing Bonfire's stamina in his determination to get out in front so early. The horses in this race were much too fast to be given such an advantage. They were holding their positions, and making Bonfire go the race of his life to get ahead of them from the outside.

Down the backstretch they went, with four colts dropping behind and moving over to the rail. But Alec saw that Tom's red-and-white silks weren't among them. Tom still wasn't ready to save ground or his colt. Bonfire continued his drive beside the three leaders. And nearing the end of the backstretch he began to push his head to the front again.

The announcer's call came, "At the far turn, it's Bonfire out in front. Lively Man on the rail is second. Third is . . ."

But Alec wasn't listening to the call. Nor did he receive any joy from seeing Bonfire in the lead. It would have been far better if Tom had dropped Bonfire back with the other colts, saving him for the long distance still to be run.

Quickly he glanced at George. The old man had his hands on his face, rubbing it, and perhaps not even seeing the race. Alec understood, for he felt the same way. His heart sickened when he saw Bonfire racing wide again going around the far turn, ahead by half a length. Yes, ahead, but at a price far greater than those closer to the rail were paying! The colt answered Tom's demand for more speed. His lightning strides came ever faster and he held his lead all around the turn.

Coming into the homestretch for the first time, it was only Lively Man who stayed with Bonfire. The roan colt had raced along the rail all the way. He was fresh compared to Bonfire, and had more speed yet to give. He came down the stretch stride for stride with the blood bay colt and they drew away from the others. Only when they passed the stands at the end of the first half-mile did Tom Messenger decide to give his colt a rest.

Alec watched him take Bonfire over to the rail behind Lively Man. His heart went out to this fighting son of the Black, who had responded so willingly to every request Tom had made of him. He wondered how much speed and stamina Bonfire had left, with another lap still to go.

George was watching the horses coming toward them.

There were tears in the old man's eyes, and his yellowed teeth pulled at his lips.

"He'll have something left for the finish," Alec told him. "I know he will."

George said nothing. He just watched.

Suddenly the crowd roared, and Alec saw Silver Knight coming down the track with a great burst of speed. The gray colt had been one of the four trailers who had tucked in close to the rail after the first turn. Now he was making his bid, moving past the two horses behind Bonfire and quickly overtaking the leaders.

The announcer called, "At the half-mile. Lively Man out in front. Bonfire is second. Silver Knight in a drive and now third, closing fast on Bonfire."

It seemed to Alec that the gray colt was almost alongside Tom before the young driver knew it. They were approaching the first turn again when Alec saw Tom glance at Silver Knight's head coming up on his right; then he asked Bonfire for more speed. It was obvious that Tom didn't want to be boxed in on the rail by the gray colt. He began to take Bonfire out from behind Lively Man. But Silver Knight's driver was determined that his bid to pass Bonfire and Lively Man was not going to be denied him. He asked his gray colt for more speed and got it.

Alec leaped to his feet when he saw Tom trying to take his colt through the small opening between Silver Knight and Lively Man. Sulky wheels were screaming hub to hub, with racing quarters dangerously close. Bonfire recoiled at the gray colt's nearness but there was no break in his long strides.

The racing horses swept into the turn. Alec's fingers

found George's shoulder and tightened. Silver Knight moved closer to Bonfire and then his sulky shaft must have struck the blood bay colt. For suddenly Bonfire jumped and there was a sickening clash as he and Silver Knight went down in a terrible huddled heap of thrashing legs and tangled sulkies.

Tail-Sitters

2

Alec's loud cry rose with those from the packed stands behind him. He knew Tom and the other driver, Ray O'Neil, were safe, for he'd seen them leap clear of their sulkies upon impact. But the colts were down.

He could do nothing until the trailing horses in the race had passed. They went wide around the turn, avoiding the fallen colts and their drivers. Alec's heart trip-hammered his chest, pounding out the seconds until finally the track was clear; then he ran forward with the grooms.

Tom and Ray O'Neil were unhurt. Both were kneeling beside their colts when Alec reached them. There was a wild, horrible fright in Bonfire's eyes as the colt attempted to lift his sweaty head.

Tom kept repeating, "Down, boy. Down." His voice broke in his terrifying concern for Bonfire. He kept his hands on the colt's head, stroking it, holding it down against the clay and sand of the track.

Alec saw at once the reason for keeping Bonfire down, although Silver Knight had been unhitched and was now being helped shakily to his feet. Sometime after his fall Bonfire had pushed his left foreleg through the wire spokes of Silver Knight's sulky wheel. The leg was held fast. If Bonfire fought to pull it free, he could easily rip a tendon and be maimed for life.

Alec dropped down beside Tom, but found he could do nothing to help.

"Easy now. Easy," Tom told Bonfire. But he knew it was only a question of seconds before the badly frightened colt would start struggling.

Someone in the crowd shouted, "He needs wire cutters. Get them from the paddock. Quick!"

Alec looked around for George. The old man was standing on the other side of Tom, his body shaking, his eyes staring and glazed. Quickly Alec went to him. *"You used wire cutters in the paddock. Did you put them back in your pocket?"*

But the old man's expression never changed, nor did he seem to hear Alec. His teeth chattered as with cold.

Alec slapped his hands against the pockets of George's overalls. He felt a hard bulge in one. Eagerly he withdrew the wire cutters and went back to Bonfire and Tom. "Keep him quiet just a second more," he said.

Tom nodded, hope coming to his eyes upon seeing the cutters. "Steady, fellow," he told Bonfire. "It's almost over."

Alec got one spoke beneath the cutters. He pressed carefully so as not to excite the colt. There was a sharp twing as the taut wire parted. Bonfire tried to raise his leg, and the wheel and battered sulky moved. He began to struggle but quieted again as Tom's hands and voice reassured him. Alec quickly cut two more spokes. Then he took hold of Bonfire's long sinewy leg and withdrew it carefully from the wheel.

They got Bonfire to his feet. No longer did his body glisten beneath the track's bright lights. The clay and sand clung heavily to his wet coat. He trembled as Alec had never seen a horse tremble before.

The track was now crowded with officials anxious to clear the way for the next race. Silver Knight had been led away some time before. The marshals closed in upon Bonfire and Tom Messenger. They got the colt moving, and Alec noticed with relief that there was no sign of lameness in Bonfire's strides.

Alec walked behind. He saw George breaking through the cordon of officials in an attempt to reach Bonfire. The old man appeared to have regained his faculties.

Alec followed them through the paddock and out the back gate. Only then did the officials disperse, leaving Tom and George alone with their colt and battered sulky. Alec caught up with them quickly, and while Tom led Bonfire, he helped George pull the sulky.

The old man was still somewhat shaken. "Thanks for what you did for him," he said.

Alec changed the subject quickly. "I think the colt's more scared than hurt," he said.

George answered, "That's what Tom thinks." The old man paused. "Well, he has every right to be scared. It wasn't pretty."

"Do you mind if I go back with you?"

George didn't look at Alec. "Of course not," he said kindly.

They went across the large, open area between the paddock and the stable area and then through another gate. Beyond were hundreds of long sheds, yellow and green beneath the lights. It was quiet here compared to the paddock and track. There were few voices, only grooms calling to one another, and the nickering of stabled horses.

They went past many sheds before stopping at one in the distant regions of the area. Alec's eyes had never left Bonfire during the long walk. No, the colt didn't show any sign of lameness. But did his fine body still tremble beneath the red-and-white cooler? A badly frightened colt could be more of a problem than a lame one.

He helped George put the sulky beneath the shed's overhang, and then he turned to Bonfire. Fear was still prominent in the colt's eyes and, when Tom removed the cooler, his body was wet and trembling. The dirt of the track hadn't had a chance to cake upon him.

Tom turned to Alec, his gaze steady and showing concern not for himself but only for his colt. "Thanks for all your help," he said.

Alec liked what he'd seen in Tom's eyes. He knew that tonight's spill wouldn't keep Tom from racing again. But Bonfire? Would the colt get over the accident as his driver had done? The answer would come when Bonfire set foot on the track again.

Tom had taken off his racing silks and was removing Bonfire's harness. George got a pail of warm water and sponges. Alec took one of the sponges and helped them wash the colt. No one said a word about the race.

Later they took turns walking the blood bay colt up and down the row, cooling him off. Alec was helping George clean the harness when the old man said, "Maybe you'd better not write Jimmy Creech about tonight."

"I wouldn't be the one to do it in any case. Jimmy is Henry's friend. I don't even know him."

"Tell Henry then," George said.

"All right." Alec finished cleaning the bridle and then said, "George—"

"Yeah?" The chaw of tobacco was shifted as the old man cocked his head to listen.

"Would it be all right with you if I stayed around?"

"Y'mean for the rest of the evening?"

"Longer than that. For a few days."

"You'd like a job?"

"Well, I've got a job but I'm not needed right now. I could stick around awhile if you'd have me."

George resumed his chewing and then said quietly, "Sure, we'll have you."

Alec turned away, watching Tom lead Bonfire toward them. Fright had left the colt's eyes. Would it reappear when he went to the track? That's what Alec wanted to know. That's why he had to stay.

"Tom," said George, "Alec's going to hang around with us for a few days."

Tom smiled, and in that smile was a sincere offer of friendship. He said, "I'm glad, Alec."

Then he turned Bonfire over to Alec, for it was his turn to walk the colt. "I don't think he's scared any more," Tom said.

"I don't think so either," Alec agreed. Beyond the row he could see the towering stands. Suddenly the lights dimmed, and a crescendo of voices could be heard above the thunderous beat of hoofs. Another race had begun. Would Bonfire ever appear on that brilliantly lighted stage again? Or get to the Hambletonian?

Later that night, Alec lay on a cot in the tack room next to Bonfire's stall. There were two other cots but only one was occupied.

"I guess Tom will be out walkin' a long while," George said in the darkness. "He's got a lot to settle with himself."

"You mean about the way he drove tonight?" Alec asked.

"Yeah, that and what's ahead of us . . . and behind us, too."

"You cover a lot of territory," Alec said with a lightness he didn't feel.

"Fifty years of it, I guess."

"I sure can't make any sense out of that, George."

"I guess not. Sometimes I don't even make sense to myself."

George was silent for a long while and Alec thought the subject had been closed; then the old man spoke again.

"The way I see it," he said, "is that Tom knows as well as I do that Jimmy's waited about fifty years to own a colt like Bonfire, one who could possibly win the Hambletonian."

George paused, and Alec heard the creak of springs as the old man suddenly sat up. "I guess I don't have to tell you what the Hambletonian means to us."

"It's your top race for three-year-olds," Alec said.

"It's more than that," George returned quickly. "It's got tradition; it's . . ." He stopped to grope for the right words to explain all that the Hambletonian meant to him. Finally he gave up and said, "Look at it this way, Alec. Give us one race to win in our lives and we'll take the Hambletonian. You have the equivalent of that in your sport."

"The Kentucky Derby," Alec said quietly. "I know what you mean, George. You don't have to explain."

"I guess not," the old man said, lying back on his pillow again. "Few of us ever come close to winning a Hambletonian. But with Bonfire Jimmy's awfully close. He knows it, I know it, and so does Tom."

"So you think that's why Tom drove as he did tonight?" Alec asked. "You think he was too anxious to make good with a top colt like Bonfire?"

"Yes, that's exactly what I mean. But not for himself or even for the colt. Tom's thinking about Jimmy. He knows Jimmy is a sick man and that he might not even get a chance to raise another colt, much less a top Hambletonian prospect."

"That's a big load for Tom to be carrying," Alec said.

"I know it and that's why I'd do anything I could for him. He's too young for that much responsibility, especially feelin' the way he does about Jimmy. But he won't listen to me. He's got a mind of his own, all right."

"How sick is Jimmy?" Alec asked. "Doesn't he come around at all to help with Bonfire's training?"

"No, he has to stay home. Doctor's orders. He had a serious operation last year and he's not supposed to get excited. Boy, he'd sure get excited around here! He hates these night raceways."

"Then how come you're here?"

"Well, that's Tom's doing, too. We've been racing Bonfire at small fairs for the past two months. That's what Jimmy wanted us to do because it's what he always did when he was driving. Bonfire had things his own way, just as any top colt would at such places. He won as he pleased with nothing ever gettin' near him. Tom decided a couple of weeks ago that it was no way to get Bonfire ready for a big race like the Hambletonian. He wrote Jimmy and got his permission to bring Bonfire here for a couple of weeks before going on to Goshen. So here we are."

Alec said bitterly, "Tonight's race sure was a good way for Bonfire to meet other top colts. It couldn't have been a worse introduction."

"I know that, all right," George agreed. "And so does Tom. That's why he's out walkin'. He must know now that he's got to set *himself* straight as well as the colt. He's got to quit thinkin' about doin' right by Jimmy. He's got to take this coming Hambletonian, big as it is, in his stride and just do the best he can. That's all Jimmy expects."

"It's easy to talk that way," Alec said. "It's something else when you're in the driver's seat."

"Sure, I know you're right, Alec. And I guess I've forgotten how it feels to be young. I suppose most fellows Tom's age would be more anxious and more eager than he is if they had a colt like Bonfire to handle."

"The chances are," Alec said, "that they wouldn't even be given a colt to train. It's usually a job for a man who's had years of colt training behind him, someone like your Jimmy Creech or my friend Henry Dailey."

The springs of George's cot groaned as he turned over. "Well, one thing is sure. Jimmy's not going to be of any help to us before we get to the Hambletonian." George paused. "How about this Henry fellow? Why don't you ask him to drop by? Maybe he could settle Tom down."

"No. I don't think Henry could make it," Alec said. "He's pretty busy."

He said nothing more and George too was silent. Alec felt sure Henry wouldn't come to any harness-racing track. He didn't care much for the sport. He'd been a jockey too long to have anything to do with people who sat behind a race-horse rather than astride one.

Henry had been very emphatic about this when Alec had called him earlier. Alec had told him of the race and accident, adding that George thought it best for him not to write Jimmy Creech about what had happened to Bonfire.

"Don't worry none about my writing him," Henry had answered. *"I'm not getting involved with Jimmy's problem or Jimmy's sport. And don't you go getting mixed up with those 'tail-sitters,' either!"*

Alec closed his eyes. He thought of Tom out walking by himself . . . and George, who was tossing restlessly on his cot, unable to sleep. He'd met them only a few hours ago and yet he seemed to know and understand them so well. He felt almost the same way about Jimmy Creech, whom he'd never even met. *Tail-sitters*, all of them. Well, he was mixed up with them, all right. And this was only the beginning.

Colt Trainer

3

Early the next morning after Bonfire had been watered and fed, George, Tom and Alec went to the track cafeteria for breakfast. Alec was the only one who ordered a large meal. George complained of stomach pains "just like the kind Jimmy used to get." Tom said he wasn't hungry.

Alec watched the young driver and trainer who was responsible for Bonfire. Tom was one of those people whose every emotion is mirrored in their eyes. And in them this morning Alec saw the same concern for Bonfire that had been there the night before, as well as a growing impatience to find out what he wanted to know.

"You'd better get some food in you," Alec suggested.

"I said I wasn't hungry," Tom answered irritably.

George looked at them. They were like a couple of yearling colts yet strikingly different in size, appearance and temperament. Tom was big and raw-boned, his gangling form promising great strength and weight in the years to come. His angular face with its high cheekbones was haggard and white despite all the days he'd spent in the sun. Its pallor was accentuated by his coal-black hair. Tom needed time to fill out, to age, before racing his best.

Alec, on the other hand, was like a compact, racy colt who had already reached his maximum strength and size. His shoulders were surprisingly large for one so young, as were his arms and chest. Only his slim hips and legs marked the boy rather than the man. Yes, George decided, Alec was like a colt who is ready to be raced. In many respects he appeared much older than Tom although his face looked more youthful. Perhaps it was his eyes that made the difference. They held all the self-confidence and maturity that Tom's lacked. No skittishness was there, and even now, when Alec was as concerned as Tom, his face retained the coloring that almost matched the red of his hair.

George ran his large-knuckled hand through the fringe of white fluff that ringed his bald dome, and decided that the safest thing for him to do was to leave Alec and Tom alone.

"Let's get out of here," Tom said. "I want to get the colt to the track."

Alec stopped eating. "Why don't you give him some time off?" he asked. "It's pretty soon after last night. He ought to be given a little chance to forget what happened."

Anger crowded out the impatience in Tom's eyes. "I'm running things, Alec," he said quickly. "If you want to stick around, okay. But leave me alone. I'll eat when I want to eat. I'll train the colt my way."

For the next few moments no one said a word.

Finally Tom pushed back his chair and got to his feet. "See you at the barn," he said. He started for the door, stopped, and turned back to Alec. "I didn't mean it the way it sounded," he apologized. "I know you're thinking of the colt too. But I've got to find out how he's going to act. You understand that, don't you, Alec?"

"Yes, I understand," Alec answered. "But I just thought you could put if off a few days. A colt forgets quickly if you give him a little time. Push him too soon, and you only run into real trouble."

"I don't have a little time," Tom returned impatiently. "I've got to find out now." He left the cafeteria.

For a few minutes Alec and George were silent. Alec toyed with his scrambled eggs without eating them, and finally pushed the plate away.

"It's strange hearing a fellow Tom's age talking about not having time," he said.

"Like I told you last night," George answered, "he's thinkin' of the Hambletonian. It's only a couple weeks off now."

"I know."

They left the cafeteria and walked through the busy stable area. Radios blared from every row while grooms worked. A voice over the public-address system tried to compete with the radios for the attention of the men.

"Fred Ringo, call long distance operator number twenty-three; that's two, three. Dr. Hunt is wanted in the race secretary's office. Ray O'Neil, call Mrs. O'Neil . . ."

Horses were already on their way to the distant training track with grooms sitting behind them and clucking. The day at Roosevelt Raceway had begun. It would end only with the turning off of the giant floodlights late that night.

George and Alec found Tom and Bonfire waiting for them. The colt had been taken from his stall and was wearing his harness. He pushed his bridled head toward Alec, nickering softly. Alec stroked him, and then helped George hitch him to the training cart. The colt was eager to go. There was no sign of lameness. His eyes were clear, devoid of any fear. As with Tom, only impatience was there. Bonfire saw the horses going to the track, and wanted to join them.

Tom said, "Okay, boy. Let's go." His words came easily, lightly. He was relieved by the way Bonfire was acting. Turning to George, he asked, "Are you coming?"

"No. I'll stay here and clean up. Take Alec along."

Tom moved over on the seat of the training cart. "C'mon, Alec. Ride over if you like."

Alec slid onto the narrow seat beside Tom, who clucked to Bonfire.

"It's good neither one of us is fat." Tom laughed.

They went across the parking lots, deserted now except for men picking up discarded papers and programs from the evening before. To the far right of the mammoth empty stands and main track was the half-mile oval used for training.

Alec noted Bonfire's pricked ears and alert head as they neared the track. The colt's red body, moving so easily between the shafts, reflected the brightness of the morning. He was everything a colt should be.

It's as though last night's accident had never been, Alec thought. *Perhaps my concern for him is needless . . . and so, perhaps, is my staying here. Henry would be much happier if I were home.*

Alec left Tom and Bonfire at the track gate, and went over to a bench and sat down. He watched Tom take the blood bay colt the wrong way around the track with other horses who were only jogging. Coming the right way around the track were the working horses, their hoofs pounding hard, their bodies lathered with sweat.

As Bonfire came around the track, Tom kept him near the outside rail, giving the other jogging horses plenty of room to pass. The blood bay colt paid no attention to those who went by. He was all business, striding easily without demanding more rein. He knew he would be asked for speed only when he was turned the right way of the track.

Watching him act so beautifully and unafraid, Alec hoped that Tom wouldn't turn him the other way this morning. If Tom would only let well enough alone for today, the colt would regain any self-confidence he might have lost by his fall. But Alec remembered Tom's remarks in the cafeteria, and knew that his was only wishful thinking.

Tom turned Bonfire around after a mile had been jogged. Alec watched him bring the colt down the center of the track. If there was going to be any trouble, it would come now, and Tom would find out all that he was so impatient to know.

Bonfire came down the homestretch without going all-out. Behind him came the faster working horses for whom Tom had left the inner rail. They moved up quickly on the blood bay colt, passing him on the inside. Bonfire paid no attention to them, nor did his strides break or falter.

After they had gone by, Tom must have given Bonfire more rein, for the colt's speed picked up. Alec knew then what Tom was doing. The horses had passed to Bonfire's left without upsetting him. Now Tom was going to take the colt past them.

Bonfire responded quickly to Tom's request for speed. He overtook those in front of him, and went by on the outside without a turn of his head.

Alec watched him draw away, going around the back

turn; then Tom began slowing him as they moved down the homestretch. Again the horses behind came up on him, but this time Tom kept Bonfire close to the inner rail.

Alec felt a heavy lump rise from his stomach to his throat. He tried swallowing to get rid of it. He watched the horses coming toward him, knowing that this was the supreme test for Bonfire. It was on his *right* that the accident had occurred the night before.

Now the others were moving up on Bonfire. A black mare was closest. Her driver began taking her past Tom, who glanced at her as she swept by. Then she was abreast of Bonfire, and the colt turned his head slightly in her direction. But there was no hesitation to his great strides.

Alec knew fleeting hope. "Go by! Go by!" he urged the mare. But then he realized that Tom must have given Bonfire more rein, for the black mare couldn't pass him. Alec's heart sickened at what Tom was asking of his colt.

Stride for stride they came, the mare's nearness making her as one with Bonfire. Tom didn't let his colt draw away from the mare. He kept Bonfire with her purposely, waiting to learn what effect the close racing quarters would have on his colt.

He found out in the next few strides. Bonfire suddenly bolted high in the air, jumping away from the mare. Tom kept his seat in the swerving cart and finally brought the colt to a stop. Like Bonfire, he was trembling.

As Alec ran toward them, he felt certain that Tom's impatience had ruined a truly great colt forever.

Together they took Bonfire back to the stables without a word to each other. Alec didn't want to speak to Tom. He was too furious with him to say anything. If he told Tom how he felt, it would only make matters worse.

Tom walked behind the blood bay colt, still holding the lines in hands that hadn't stopped shaking since he had brought Bonfire to a halt. His face disclosed all his misery. Disappointment was there. And although impatience had left his eyes, insecurity and helplessness were evident there now. Tom knew he had a real problem on his hands, and he didn't know how to cope with it.

At the stables George didn't have to ask them how things had gone. He had only to look at their faces to know. He helped to unhitch Bonfire and then sponged him down. When he had finished he put a cooler over the colt and looked around. Only Alec was there, and he was cleaning the harness.

"I'll do that job," George said, "if you walk him. My legs are botherin' me today."

"Sure," Alec said. The colt had stopped trembling and the fright had left his eyes. But after this morning's incident it would take a fine colt trainer to rid Bonfire of his fear. It had become a living part of him.

Suddenly George spoke. "Did Tom push him too hard?"

Alec nodded. "Bonfire was doing all right until then."

An hour later Alec was still walking the colt when Tom joined him. They walked on either side of Bonfire in silence.

"Want me to take him now?" Tom asked after a few minutes.

"I don't mind walking him. He's just about dry, anyway." Alec wasn't angry with Tom any longer. After all, Tom wasn't to blame. The person at fault was Jimmy Creech—the man who'd given Tom the great responsibility of training a young, high-strung colt.

Tom said, "I don't have to tell you that you were right . . . I mean about what you said in the cafeteria at breakfast."

Alec stopped Bonfire so that he might see the boy on the other side. "Tom," he said, "I don't know any more about this than you do. Colt training isn't for us. It's a job for experienced men. It's a skill that's acquired only after many years of trial and error. When things go right for a colt, the job's hard enough. If anything goes wrong, it calls for the very best of horsemen."

Tom turned away. "What you're driving at," he said in a voice barely above a whisper, "is that things have gone wrong and you can't help me. No one can."

"You need Jimmy Creech," Alec said. It was no time for anything but frankness.

Tom shook his head. "No, I couldn't do that. It's the last thing I'd ever do. He's sick enough as it is. The operation he had last fall wasn't as successful as we thought."

Alec turned Bonfire around and took him back to the stall. The colt tossed his head, and then got down and rolled in the straw. Alec and Tom watched him for a long while without saying a word. Finally Bonfire got up and came close to them, pushing his mole-soft nose into their shirt pockets.

Tom got a carrot for him. While Bonfire was eating it, Tom said, "You told us about Henry Dailey, who's Jimmy's old friend. Wouldn't he help me with Bonfire? Could you ask him, Alec?"

"He wouldn't come, Tom. He doesn't like harness racing very much."

"But he likes colts, doesn't he?"

"Of course," Alec said.

"He might do it for Jimmy," Tom urged.

"I doubt it, Tom. You see . . ."

"Please, Alec. Phone him. Ask him to come down just for a day, just to tell me what to do. I've *got* to get Bonfire to the Hambletonian."

Alec studied Tom for many seconds and then said, "All right, Tom. We'll try it. Come on."

A few minutes later Tom stood outside the open door of the telephone booth, waiting while Alec's call to Henry was put through. Finally the call was completed.

"It's Alec, Henry."

"Hello, Alec. Y'coming home?"

"No, not just yet."

"When then? You're not getting mixed up with those guys, are you?"

Before answering, Alec looked at Tom, knowing the boy could hear every word Henry spoke in his loud, ringing voice. But it was too late to back down.

"In a way," Alec finally said.

"What way?"

"It's the colt, Henry. Bonfire acted up on the track this morning. He's scared of anything coming up on his right. We need help with him. He's scheduled to go in the Hambletonian."

Alec waited, but there was no sound from the other end. "Henry, did you hear me? Are you still there?"

"Yeah, I'm still here, Alec."

"He's a wonderful colt, Henry. You'd love him as much as I do, if you saw him."

"Don't worry, I won't."

"What was that, Henry?"

"I said, don't worry, I won't see him."

Alec glanced at Tom. "That's what I thought you said."

"You'd better come home, Alec, an' leave that sport alone. It's for Jimmy Creech and his kind, not for us."

"Henry—"

"Yes, Alec?"

"How often have you told me that loving horses means loving any kind of horse, regardless of type or breed or the use to which he is put? How many hundreds of times, Henry?" There was a sharpness to Alec's voice that hadn't been there before.

Henry knew Alec was angry with him. "What's that got to do with it?" he asked challengingly.

"You know as well as I do," Alec said simply.

"Well, what is it that you want me to do?" Henry bellowed.

"I'd like you to come here and . . ."

Before Alec had finished his sentence, Henry said louder than before, "I won't have anything to do with that kind of horse. I told you that when you left here. I tell you that again."

"That *kind*, Henry? Aren't you forgetting that he's a son of the Black?"

"But his dam is a harness-racing mare. *That* makes the difference." Henry had control of himself again. He was no longer shouting into the phone.

"But it was you who arranged the mating," Alec said, refusing to give up. "You had Jimmy Creech send his mare to the Black."

"I did it as a favor to an old friend. It doesn't mean that I have to like his kind of racing."

"No one's asking you to like it," Alec said bitterly. "We're just asking you for help with *his* colt."

"Let Jimmy figure it out. He's good at that."

"He's a sick man. You know that from his letter."

"He'll get someone to take over the colt, Alec. Don't you worry none about that. And whoever Jimmy gets will do a better job than I could." He paused, and then added, "—or you can do either, Alec. Better come home. It's no business of ours."

Alec knew he was beaten. He spoke barely above a whisper as he said, "It *is* our business, Henry. I'm staying on. Goodbye." He hung up, not knowing if Henry had heard him, and not really caring.

Tom moved away from the door when Alec came out of the booth. Together they walked back to the stables and Bonfire without saying a word.

The Blind

4

Tom and Alec didn't take Bonfire to the track the next day. Instead they let him rest and during the late afternoon took him out to graze.

Tom held the lead shank, and let Bonfire choose his own patches of grass. Alec walked a little behind, content to be with them rather than with George, who had tried all day long to relieve the tension by a constant flow of small talk.

Alec watched Bonfire's smooth muscles slide easily beneath his flaming red coat while he moved from one patch of green to the next. *His coat* should *look good,* Alec thought. *We've each groomed him several times today, trying to keep ourselves from thinking too much.*

Finally Bonfire reached the far end of the grassy area. Just beyond was some fine sand. He tugged a little on the lead shank, and Tom let him go. Reaching the sand, Bonfire lowered his small head, sniffing and blowing the fine grains. He was as particular here as he'd been with his choice of

40

grass. For many seconds he moved about the sand before finding the spot he liked best. Then he very carefully bent his forelegs and then his hind legs, lowering himself into the sand and swinging over on his back.

"There goes our grooming," Tom said, smiling.

Bonfire rolled from side to side, kicking his black-stockinged legs in the air and grunting in his great pleasure. After a few minutes he got up on all fours again, the sand clinging to his tall body.

Tom said, "All day long I've been thinking without getting anywhere. I don't know what to do about him."

Alec confessed, "I've been trying to decide what Henry would do, if he were here."

Eagerly Tom sought Alec's help. "What do you think he'd do?"

"I guess he'd leave him alone awhile, and then gradually start working him with other horses until he regained his confidence."

Disappointment flooded Tom's eyes and he said quickly, "We couldn't do anything like that and still get him to the Hambletonian. It would take too long."

"Yes," Alec admitted, "it would. Henry doesn't believe in rushing a colt."

"But if he *had* to?" There was desperation in Tom's voice. "If he had *my* problem of having to get Bonfire to race here, and then go on to the Hambletonian?"

"Is racing here so important?"

"He needs it, Alec. He needs the tightening up such a race would give him. That's why we came here."

"He'd be better off if you hadn't," Alec said, and immediately regretted his thoughtless words. He turned away quickly. "I'm sorry, Tom," he apologized. "I didn't mean that as a criticism of you."

Tom didn't answer. He took Bonfire back to the grass, and let him graze again.

Alec followed them. Trying to make amends and be helpful he said, "I think I know what Henry might do if he had *our* problem, Tom."

The boy turned to him once more.

Alec went on, "I believe he'd put a blind over his right eye. Henry doesn't like to use mechanical aids, but if he *had* to, I guess he would."

"Bonfire couldn't see what was beside him, wearing a blind," Tom considered thoughtfully. "Yes, I guess Jimmy might do something like that too, although I've never seen him use one. He likes a horse to go clean and free of anything but an open bridle."

Alec said, "I wouldn't make it a closed blind so Bonfire couldn't see anything out of his right eye. I don't think he'd like that."

Tom was eager now and hopeful. "Yeah. Sure. I think you're right," he said. "Just a partial blind, one that keeps him from seeing what's behind and directly on his right. But he'll be able to see what's in front. That shouldn't bother him any."

"No, it shouldn't," Alec agreed. "We can try it and see. If it works you can go ahead and race him here."

Tom took Bonfire by the halter and began leading the colt back to the stables. "We'll try it on him tomorrow morning."

Alec fell in beside him. "Tom," he said, "there's one other thing I'd like you to do, if you will."

"Sure. What is it, Alec?"

"Try to get someone you know around here to let me take a horse tomorrow. I'd like to go alongside you and Bonfire."

Tom said, "Sure, Alec, if that's what you want to do."

Tom talked about their plans for the following day all the way back to the stables, but Alec said nothing more. He hoped that what he'd suggested would work out well, but he wasn't certain of it.

The sun rose hot and red the next morning, burnishing Bonfire's body when they took him from his stall. He wore his new bridle with the thin piece of leather that bulged about his right eye, preventing him from seeing to the rear or to the side. Late the afternoon before, they had walked him about while he'd gotten used to it.

George had shaken his head miserably when he'd seen the blind. After having worked for Jimmy Creech for more than thirty years, he knew how his friend felt about such things.

Now George helped Tom hitch Bonfire, while Alec stood beside the brown gelding Tom had managed to get from a trainer up the row. Feeling more miserable than ever, George glanced at Tom, hoping desperately that the boy knew what he was doing. Tom was like a son to him, and he felt more concerned about him than about Bonfire or Jimmy. The kid was taking everything he had to do terribly hard. It wasn't right. It could lead to trouble.

They finished hitching Bonfire, and Tom called to Alec, "All set!" He slid into the seat behind the blood bay colt and then turned to George. "Are you coming over this morning?"

"Yeah," the old man said, "I guess I will."

Alec drove his brown gelding ahead of Bonfire on the way to the track. He didn't think much of his charge as a race-horse. In fact, he was certain this one hadn't done any rac-ing. The gelding was too heavily built and bad-gaited. His mouth was like a piece of lead, and Alec had to use all his skill in getting him to do what he wanted. But the gelding would serve the purpose of the morning's work.

He stopped his horse at the track gate, letting Bonfire pass them.

"We'll jog a mile," Tom called, "and then turn."

Alec nodded, and followed Bonfire up the homestretch. The blood bay colt was going beautifully, not objecting at all to his blind. Alec felt his hopes rise. Perhaps it *was* going to be a successful aid.

But he didn't look at Bonfire too often going around the track, for his brown horse kept him very busy. Alec worked the bit constantly in the gelding's hard mouth, teaching him to have respect for the hands that guided him. Fortunately Alec had ridden many horses like him and he found there was little difference when sitting behind one.

By the time they had finished their mile jog, Alec had complete control over the brown horse. But he was more thankful than ever for the years of riding that had developed the strength in his back, shoulders and arms. Here was no racing machine, whose speed could be turned on and off by slight commands, but a horse who had respect only for strength.

Tom didn't turn Bonfire around until a group of fast-working horses went by. Alec followed, giving Bonfire plenty of room. Together they started down the homestretch with Alec far to the right and a little behind Bonfire. Tom glanced at him and called to him to move the brown horse over to the left.

Alec shook his head and kept the gelding in the center of the track. There was time enough to move closer to Bonfire. He waited until they were in the backstretch and he was certain that the heavy sound of the gelding's hoofs wouldn't disturb Bonfire; then he began taking his horse across the track.

Tom watched Alec come closer. He watched Bonfire too. The colt seemed to be paying no attention to the horse coming up on his right. Bonfire could not see the gelding but certainly he could hear him. His long strides came smoothly, easily. His head was high and pushed forward. He was asking for more rein but not demanding it.

Tom felt certain the blind was a success. He called to Alec to take the gelding past Bonfire.

They went around the back turn before Alec made his move. The brown horse's heavy hoofs moved a bit sluggishly before Alec got more speed from him and sent him past Tom and then alongside Bonfire. As a team they started down the homestretch, the two horses going stride for stride, and head for head. One second, two seconds, three seconds—and Bonfire never broke stride.

Alec knew then that the blind was working. Yet there was one more move to be made before he could be sure it was a complete success. He had to take his horse past Bonfire, so that the colt would be able to see him when he got a little to the front. But Alec was certain the worst was over, that Bonfire wouldn't object to seeing a horse to his right and just *ahead* of him. He had told this to Tom the day before.

He began to move the brown gelding past Bonfire. Little

by little he went ahead until the colt was able to see him. Then everything happened so quickly that Alec was never sure of the true sequence of events.

Suddenly Bonfire took a mighty leap, scaring the brown gelding, who jumped too. Alec fought for control when his horse broke from his hands and swerved across the track before straightening out. Bonfire was running directly ahead of them. But the seat of the cart was empty.

Then Alec saw Tom, stretched out on the track before them. He tried desperately to pull his horse away *but it was too late.* He heard the thud of shod hoofs on flesh. Then the cart lurched as a wheel went over Tom. As Alec slumped weakly in his seat, the last thing he remembered seeing was Tom's face with the mouth open slightly as though the boy were pleading with him not to let the horse hit him—and Tom's hand raised in a pitiful attempt to ward off the on-coming hoofs.

The New Arrival

5

Later Alec found himself back at the stables, stripping Bonfire of his harness. Everything he did came automatically, requiring no mental effort. He thought only of Tom's inert body being carried from the track and placed flat in the back of someone's car. George had gone with Tom to the nearby hospital.

Alec hoped desperately that Tom was going to be all right. He washed Bonfire and then began walking him. It was now mid-morning, with a blistering sun beating down upon them. Yet Alec felt terribly cold. He shivered with chill and walked the blanketed colt faster. Finally he broke into a half-run and Bonfire trotted beside him. Suddenly he realized what he was doing and came to an abrupt stop. The stable area was unusually quiet.

Alec knew that the reason he had run was that he was trying to get away from the mental picture of Tom lying on the track. But he knew too that it did him no good to run. He went forward again, walking slowly.

47

For an hour more he walked Bonfire, fighting the thoughts thrusting themselves into his consciousness. First, he told himself that Tom wasn't hurt badly. Maybe a sprained shoulder. Maybe not even that. Tom would be back with them by . . . well, maybe tomorrow. But this reasoning did not help. He knew he was only fooling himself. There was no telling how much injury the gelding's heavy hoofs had done. He could only pray that they had missed Tom's head.

Alec took Bonfire back to his stall and then went to the tack room, where he lay down on his cot. He told himself that accidents like this happened sometimes. It was horse racing. It was the chance every jockey and every driver took every day, many times a day. It wasn't surprising that accidents happened. What really was surprising was that they didn't happen more often. He knew this. He had accepted it years ago. Everyone in the sport accepted it, Tom included.

Alec's eyes rested on Tom's cot, rumpled and unmade, just as the boy had left it early that morning when he'd been so eager to get to the track to try out the new blind.

Alec rose from his cot and hurriedly left the room. He walked aimlessly about the stable area, seeing nothing, hearing nothing. If only he hadn't suggested the blind. If only he'd let Tom and Bonfire alone.

An empty cardboard box lay in his path. He kicked it viciously, watching it turn over in the air and come down.

"Go ahead, kick yourself around too," he told himself bitterly. "But it won't do any good. It won't help Tom."

Alec walked faster and faster until he was almost in a run. Sometimes he was able to drive Tom's face from his mind. But most of the time it was there before him, just as it had been on the track—so pale, so pleading. And subconsciously he kept repeating, "I did it to him. I lost control of my horse or it wouldn't have happened. Because I can ride I thought I could *drive*. I insisted upon getting out there with him. I wanted to help and instead I blundered terribly. I've made things worse than they'd ever have been if I'd left him alone. I did it to him. I'm responsible."

Later he went back to the stall and stayed with Bonfire. He groomed the colt, trying not to think and just waiting for George to return. Finally a voice from the doorway said, "I'm back, Alec."

The brush fell from his hand. He picked it up and then turned to George, his eyes asking the question he wanted to have answered.

"He's got a broken leg," George said. "Nothing more." He studied Alec for many seconds and then added, "It could have been a lot worse. Don't take it so hard."

"I know," Alec answered. "I was so afraid we'd hit him in the head."

"Something knocked him out but not the gelding's hoofs. Maybe it was the cart. I don't know. Anyway he's not bad off, considering everything."

Alec left Bonfire's side and went over to George. Tom was going to be all right. That's what he'd hoped for. Now he'd be able to get rid of that awful mental picture. He'd never hurt anyone before. He'd taken plenty of spills himself but this had been different, very different.

The two stood in the doorway, their eyes on the blood bay colt.

George said, "Bonfire's goin' home, Alec. There won't be any Hambletonian for him."

"Or for Tom or Jimmy," Alec heard himself add quietly. And then he wondered why he didn't offer to race Bonfire. Wouldn't he have done so under any other circumstances?

George said, "Yeah, it's goin' to be tough on Jimmy, all right, but it's a lot worse for Tom. He'll be laid up for at least three months."

"Is that what they said?"

George nodded. "The doctor recommended that Tom be taken to a Pittsburgh hospital so he'll be near home. The doc's contacted a fine bone specialist who'll do the operatin'."

"Operate?" Alec asked, startled. "Can't they set it without operating?"

"The thigh bone is broken. The doc said it's the most important bone in the body—it carries most of the weight. They'll operate and put in a temporary pin. It'll mean Tom won't have to wear a heavy body cast while the bone is healin'. He'll be able to get around with crutches. He's pretty happy about that."

Alec thought bitterly, *I'll bet he's happy. I'll bet he feels just swell. The poor guy.*

George went on, "So I'm flyin' to Pittsburgh with him tomorrow. We get an ambulance at both ends, an' all the arrangements have been made. But I'm stayin' with him to make sure everything goes just as they say it will. Tom's not goin' through this alone. Not with me around, he isn't."

"What about Bonfire?" Alec wanted to know. "How's he getting back, George?"

"I've already hired a guy to drive our van back with him."

"And Jimmy?" Alec asked. "Have you called him?"

"I'm doin' that right away." George went to Bonfire and

gently rubbed the colt's head. "Looks like we're all goin' to be turned out to pasture for a while," he told Bonfire. "Next year maybe things will work out better for us. 'Course you'll be too old for the Hambletonian, but you got to take the bad with the good. Jimmy will see it that way, I know."

Alec watched the old man and the colt, but said nothing.

George asked, "I guess you'll be goin' home, Alec, won't you?"

"Yes. There's no reason for my staying now." Alec lowered his gaze to the straw bedding. Was it over for him too? Was he any different from what he'd been before coming to Roosevelt Raceway, before meeting Bonfire and Tom and George? Or even before the accident?

Alec turned to Bonfire again. He didn't like this continual gnawing inside him. He didn't like the way he felt at all.

He loved Bonfire. Why then didn't he ask to take over this colt? Probably Jimmy Creech wouldn't let him do it. But at least why didn't he ask? Was he afraid to train and race Bonfire? Of course not. He'd never been afraid to race *any* horse. But before this morning he'd never hurt anyone, either.

Again Alec was conscious of the tightness within his chest. He wanted to shout to George that *he had to race Bonfire.* But he could say nothing.

A moment later he heard a familiar voice, one that was warm and friendly and casual. "I can't figure you out, Alec. You ask me to come and I come. Then the minute I get here you say you're goin' home."

Alec turned and looked at the short, broad-shouldered man leaning comfortably against the stall door. No longer could he keep his feelings to himself, and especially not from somebody he had known and worked with for so many years. Henry Dailey could almost read his mind. But all Alec said was, "You're a little late, Henry."

Henry smiled and came inside, his bowlegs taking him quickly over the straw. "Never too late," he said, holding out his hand to George. "Hello, George. My name's Dailey." He nodded toward Bonfire, adding, "I've been standin' outside lookin' at him while you fellows been talkin'. A grand colt, a beautiful colt, just like you said, Alec."

Removing his battered hat, Henry ran a handkerchief over the top of his brow and through his long white hair. "A scorcher," he said, turning to George again. "This is the kind of a day when you ought to be thankful you got no hair to make you hotter, George."

The old groom frowned and shifted his tobacco chaw from one side of his mouth to the other. George didn't like to be reminded of his baldness. Nor did he like the way this man took over the stall, so casual, so confident.

Alec too was impressed by Henry's attitude. It was as though nothing unusual had happened, as if Henry dropped around to Roosevelt Raceway every day.

Henry replaced his hat. "Let's get a cup of coffee and talk, Alec," he said. Outside the stall he stopped and looked back at Bonfire. His eyes were still on the colt when he said, "George, I wonder if you'd mind puttin' off your phone call to Jimmy until we get back? I'd like to talk to him too. I got a feelin' Alec and me won't be goin' home."

All the way to the cafeteria, Henry maintained an incessant stream of small talk. Sitting down at the table, his coffee before him, he said, "You're sure you don't want anything to eat, Alec? Have you had lunch?"

Alec shook his head. "I'm not hungry. I'll get something later on."

"Everything's fine back at the farm," Henry said. "That War Admiral mare is over her cold. I had the vet give her the terramycin shots like you said to do. The only trouble with usin' those drugs is that they cost too darn much. Our bill from the vet alone the past few months is almost as much as what it would cost us to buy another good broodmare."

Alec said, "It's better than losing our horses."

"Yeah. Sure. I'm with you a hundred percent. You know that, Alec. All I mean is that we've had more than our share of sick horses this year." He paused before adding, "The Black is sure feelin' good. But he misses you, Alec."

Henry finished his coffee and went to get another cup. When he came back he talked about Roosevelt Raceway for the first time. His voice and manner didn't change. Both held the same casualness as before. "I looked at the horses here while I was tryin' to find you, Alec. They're a lot different from what they used to be. If harness racin' has changed so have the horses." Henry chuckled. "Why, I remember my father unhitchin' his mare from a plow and takin' her into town for an afternoon of racin'. There was nothin' unusual about that in the old days. It was what was expected of harness-racin' horses, an' they were built for it."

Henry turned to look out the window in the direction of the stables. "I guess I shouldn't be so surprised at the change in them after all the years I been away from this sport. They're a racy bunch now an' I can't see any of 'em pullin' plows. They're built for speed, not work." He chuckled again. "But did I expect harness racin' to stand still any more than our own sport? These horses are the result of careful line breeding. Some of 'em are just as fine-boned as anything I've seen at our tracks."

Alec said, "I thought you'd like Bonfire."

"Yeah, I was includin' him, all right. He's racier than any of 'em. There's a lot of the Black in that colt. No mistake about that." Henry paused and for the first time his eyes and voice lost their lightness. "But don't get the idea from what I've said that this sport's for me. I want no part of it except to help you with Bonfire."

Alec looked up. "Is that why you came?"

"Of course. I felt pretty bad after your phone call the other day. When I didn't feel any better about it this morning, I hopped into the car and came down."

Alec's gaze shifted uneasily. "As I said a little while ago, you're too late, Henry. Tom's in the hospital. Bonfire's going home."

"He's not goin' home, not after I get through talkin' to Jimmy," Henry said emphatically. "Don't you worry about that none. Let's talk about you and Tom. What happened out there this morning?"

Alec told him as quickly and simply as he could. He didn't look at Henry but he knew his friend's eyes were focused on him.

When Alec had finished Henry said, "As George said back there, it could have been a lot worse. Tom will be all right. Forget about him for a while, Alec."

"It's not that easy."

"I know," Henry said understandingly, "but you'll manage it."

"I never hurt anyone before, Henry. It's not like taking

the fall myself. This is different, somehow. It's hard to explain."

"You don't have to explain. I know how you feel, Alec. We'll lick it all right." Henry paused. Then he said, "Let's not talk about it any more. Let's get back to the colt. He can't talk, so we'll have to figure out for ourselves what we're up against."

For more than an hour they discussed Bonfire. Afterward Alec felt much better. He got something to eat, and when he'd finished said, "Everything seems different with you here, Henry. I know you'll be able to help him."

The old trainer said, "Maybe I will and maybe I won't. All I can do is give him a chance to regain his self-confidence. If he has the courage to come back an' the will to race again, he'll make it all by himself. I'll just be doin' the groundwork."

There was hope in Alec's voice as he said, "That's all he needs. He'll come back strong. He's one of the good ones."

"You should know, Alec," Henry said, turning away. "I'm sure you're right." He finished his coffee, well aware that he wasn't certain at all that he could do anything for Bonfire in so short a time before the Hambletonian. Nor was he any more certain about Alec. Both of them needed time, and he wasn't being given much of it. "Let's get out of here, Alec," he said finally. "We got a lot to do."

They went back to the stables, and found George packing his suitcase. He turned around when they entered the tack room, his face grave in his concern for Tom and for what was ahead of him. Yet when he saw Henry a slight flicker of defiance showed in his eyes. He knew this man wasn't one of them. He didn't have to be told; he sensed it all by himself.

And after having worked for Jimmy Creech so many years, he didn't like Henry's cocky assurance, either.

Henry said, "Alec and I are stayin' here, George. That's what I want to tell Jimmy. We want to take over the colt."

George looked at Alec sympathetically, and then his gaze shifted to Bonfire's tack trunk, which he'd already packed and closed. "I spoke to Jimmy a few minutes ago," he told Henry. "I couldn't wait for you any longer."

An angry crimson flush swept over Henry's face.

George broke the tense silence by closing his suitcase and saying, "Jimmy said to send the colt home just as I'd arranged. He's meeting Tom and me at the Pittsburgh airport."

Trying to keep the anger out of his voice, Henry asked, "Did you tell him I was here and wanted to talk to him?"

"No," George said.

"Then you'd better come with me now while I call him," Henry said, taking George by the arm and moving him toward the door. "I want you to hear what he has to say so you'll know it's all right to leave Bonfire with us."

Alec watched them go. George had stopped struggling. Now he was even walking ahead of Henry as though eager to make the phone call and have Jimmy put this *intruder* in his proper place.

Alec went to Bonfire. The colt had his head over the half-door and Alec rubbed him softly behind the ears. It might happen that he would be with this colt only a little while longer. He hoped not. He hoped Jimmy would agree to leave Bonfire behind. Alec knew that with Henry's help he and Bonfire would get to the Hambletonian.

Almost an hour went by before Henry and George returned. Alec needed only to look at their faces to know how much the long talk with Jimmy Creech had taken from both men. Their faces were taut and white with nervous fatigue. Henry had been given charge of Bonfire. Alec knew this from the pinpoints of light in his friend's eyes. He pulled the colt's head a little closer to let him know.

George was not angry but tolerant and submissive. Jimmy's decision had relieved him of all responsibility for Bonfire. Now his only concern was for Tom. "I'll go and tell the van driver not to come around tomorrow morning," he said.

Henry stopped before the stall, putting a large hand on Bonfire. Alec noticed that it was trembling.

"How'd it go?" he asked.

"Rough," Henry answered. "Jimmy was never very easy to get along with. He's worse now. Maybe it's because he's been so sick. He has a mind of his own, and he flares up worse than the worst kind of young colt." Henry paused, his face relaxing a little while he looked at Bonfire. "But we got this fellow anyway," he added. "Jimmy's got too much at stake not to take any kind of a chance . . . *even on me*."

"Doesn't he like you?" Alec asked.

"Sure he likes me, or we wouldn't have his colt," Henry snapped back. "And I like Jimmy too. It's just that we don't think alike. We never did." Henry paused. "But I don't want to talk about him any more. Enough is enough."

They stood quietly beside the stall for a few more minutes and then Henry said, "When George gets back I want you and me to go over to the hospital."

Alec felt his face stiffen. Finally he said, "Sure, Henry. I want to see Tom before he leaves."

It was going to be difficult, Alec knew, seeing Tom in the hospital and knowing what lay ahead of him before he'd be able to walk again. Henry must be well aware of this. Perhaps that's why he had suggested the visit. Henry wanted him to face what he'd done to Tom, *and then forget it.*

Henry had taken over.

The Long Chance

6

Alec slept very little that night. He tossed restlessly on his cot, knowing that Henry was wide-awake too. And yet he was able to close his eyes without seeing Tom's face on the track before him. His visit to the hospital had done that for him.

They'd been given only five minutes with Tom. Nothing was as difficult as Alec had thought it would be. At first it had been hard, walking into the room and seeing Tom's leg held high by traction weights. But Tom said he had no pain, that the traction wasn't as bad as it probably looked to them. He was anxious to get to Pittsburgh and have the operation done. He was glad he wasn't going to need a body cast, for it would have kept him in bed. He'd be up and around again soon, using crutches. He was going to make very sure he'd be up in time to fly with Jimmy to see the Hambletonian. He wasn't going to miss that, even if he had to walk all the way to Goshen, New York.

When they'd left Tom, Henry had said, "You don't have

to worry none about that boy. He's game as they come. Nothin's going to keep him from racing horses again, especially nothin' like a broken leg."

Alec turned over on his cot. They couldn't fail Tom. He'd been so happy and pleased when they'd told him Bonfire wasn't being sent home. No, none of them could let Tom down.

This was George's last night with them, and the alarm clock had been set for an early hour. As it turned out, George didn't need to be awakened by the alarm, for Henry was up before dawn.

George heard him, and immediately got out of bed and dressed. Then he went over to Alec's cot. "You awake, Alec?"

"Yes, George. Are you going now?"

"Might as well. It's earlier than I'd planned, but so much the better. I'll reach the hospital in good time."

From outside they heard Bonfire's low nicker.

"Does Henry get up this early every morning?" George asked, picking up his suitcase.

"At the track he does. He stays in bed longer at home."

George said, "It's not goin' to make him very popular around here. They put out the track lights and quit work only a few hours ago."

Alec swung himself to a sitting position on the side of his cot. "Not being popular won't bother Henry any," he said.

George groped for Alec's hand in the darkness. "I guess I don't have to tell you how much I'm hopin' for the best for you an' the colt . . . and Henry," he added thoughtfully.

"Thanks, George. You take care of Tom. Make sure everything goes right."

"I will. Good-bye, Alec."

"Good-bye, George."

After the old man had left, Alec dressed, putting on the clean jeans and sweatshirt that Henry had thoughtfully brought along. He felt a lot better for having them. They were as clean and fresh as the morning itself. He was eager to get to work before the sun came up.

The sky was a dull gray when Alec returned from the washroom. He found Henry grooming Bonfire. "George says you're not going to be very popular around here," he said, smiling.

"That's what he told me," Henry replied as he went on with his work. "I've never seen such a place. After five, and no one's up but us."

"Their schedule isn't the same as ours, Henry."

The trainer cleaned the straw from Bonfire's long black tail. "So much the better for what we got to do," he said.

Alec glanced at him in a puzzled manner and then shrugged his shoulders. He'd know soon enough what Henry had in mind.

The colt tossed his head, pulling at the tie ropes. He nickered, and from along the row came the answers of other horses. A sleepy, angry voice shouted, "Quiet, *you*!"

Henry said, "I'm goin' to take Bonfire for a little walk an' get to know him better. You can clean up the stall if you like. I'll be back as soon as it gets light enough for us to see on the track."

Alec nodded, and went to work. He hadn't figured on going to the track this morning. He'd thought Henry would give the colt a day off.

Later Henry came back with the colt. "Let's hook him up

now," he said. "Bonfire told me he likes getting out this early."

Alec pushed the training cart from under the overhang, while Henry put on the colt's bridle. It was an open bridle, Alec noticed. No blind for Bonfire today. And the colt was eager to go, just as Henry had said.

Alec watched Henry tighten the harness leather about the shafts. His hands worked expertly, never fumbling or groping. Regardless of how Henry felt about harness racing he knew what he was doing.

Alec had taken up the long lines when Henry said, "We're just going to jog a little this morning. I want to see his action, an' I also want to see how he goes with an open bridle." He turned from the colt to Alec. "In other words, I'm startin' at the beginning this morning. No one will be out on the track with you, an' like I said, that's better for us. I don't want to put him in any kind of a tight spot this morning. I'll learn all I want to know just by watchin' the two of you."

Alec slid into the seat behind Bonfire and moved to the far side. "I guess you could ride over, if you wanted," he suggested.

"No thanks," Henry answered quietly. "I'm not *that* keen about bein' here."

Bonfire began moving, and Alec lifted his dangling feet to the iron stirrups on the shafts. The colt strode easily without demanding more rein. His tail came back, flicking Alec in the face.

Tail-sitter, that's what I am now, Alec thought. He glanced back at Henry, wondering how his old friend felt about seeing him behind a colt rather than astride one.

Alec slowed Bonfire to a walk while crossing the macadam road that led to the huge parking area. Beyond, the great stands loomed black and grotesque in the early-morning grayness. Alec turned the colt toward the training track, letting him go into his fast walk. He was glad they'd have the track to themselves.

He clucked to Bonfire as they went up the homestretch. He felt the slightly stronger pull on the lines, now that the colt had the track beneath his hoofs. But Bonfire requested rather than demanded more rein. He had a very light mouth, and was most obedient and responsive. Like Satan back at home, Bonfire's speed could be turned on and off by Alec's slightest commands.

Alec sat back comfortably in his seat. He hummed a little, glorying in being alone with a fine colt on a fine morning. It was a world set apart from all others, and his love for it drove everything else from his mind.

They completed one lap, passing Henry, who sat on a bench near the middle of the homestretch. But Alec was too happy to notice Henry's close scrutiny as they went by. Even so it wouldn't have mattered, for it was what he expected of Henry.

Alec kept humming to his colt, feeling relaxed and very much at home. He knew he needed to give Bonfire only the lightest touch and the speed would come. But he kept him to the slow jog Henry had ordered and completed another lap.

Going around the track for the third time, he saw another horse coming through the gate. He felt his spine stiffen, and then was able to relax again. But his gaze shifted often to the horse jogging around the far turn behind them.

As he took Bonfire into the homestretch, approaching Henry again, his eyes sought the trainer, asking him what he wanted done. The horse behind was coming along at a faster clip than Bonfire. Soon he'd be overtaking them.

"Keep going, Alec," Henry called, waving them on.

Alec nodded and continued up the track. But nothing was the same as it had been before. He felt tense. He kept looking back at the horse jogging behind them, coming ever closer.

Henry rose from his seat on the bench, strode a few feet, and then sat down again. "Use your eyes, not your feet!" he told himself angrily. He had seen Alec stiffen in the cart seat. And now he watched him glance back often at the horse coming around the turn. It wasn't like Alec to pay attention to anything but his own horse.

Henry's gaze left Alec for the man driving the horse down the stretch. When he went by, the man called, "Howdy! Nice morning."

"Howdy," answered Henry. "Sure is."

Then he looked on ahead at Bonfire and Alec. He had only to watch the colt to know that Alec was tense. Bonfire was a highly strung, sensitive colt. He felt everything his driver did. He had a mouth that turned those leather lines into electric wires. And through them Alec's uneasiness was being transmitted to the colt.

Henry's eyes narrowed with concern. He turned and looked back at the horse behind, so far behind that Bonfire didn't know he was being followed. The colt's restlessness was all Alec's doing. Alec and his turning head.

Henry thought, *It might be worse for Alec than I'd figured on. I can't believe it, though. Alec's never been afraid of anything. He isn't now. Not for himself, anyway. He's afraid of what the colt might do. He doesn't want to hurt anyone again. But he's not making it any easier for the colt or himself . . . or for me. I'm stuck here, all right, whether I like it or not. We're not going to take this home with us. I got to lick it where it started, and that's right on a harness track.*

Henry watched the other horse draw ever closer to Bonfire. They came down the backstretch, around the turn, and toward him again. He saw Alec glance at him, expecting a signal to stop the colt rather than go around again. But Henry waved them on for another lap.

There was nothing for Alec to be concerned about, Henry knew. The horse coming up would pass far to Bonfire's right. Their colt couldn't possibly become scared with so much running room. Alec must know this, but he just didn't want to take any chances.

Henry kept his eyes on Bonfire while the other horse moved by, with his driver calling "Howdy" to Alec. Henry noticed the turning of Bonfire's head to the right and his increased nervousness. But, just as he'd expected, the colt didn't break stride and kept right on going.

Henry's eyes followed them around the track once more. With a little time he could have restored Bonfire's confidence in himself without resorting to any mechanical aids. But he didn't have the time if they were to race here. So he had to think of something that would help the colt to keep his mind on racing. Alec needed it as much as Bonfire. Fix the colt, and he'd fix Alec. A big order in a hurry. But it had to be done.

Henry motioned to Alec to bring Bonfire to a stop at the track gate. He walked beside him all the way back to the stables, saying very little.

Later, when Bonfire had been cooled out and put back in

his stall, Alec said, "You haven't told me much, Henry."

"I know. I've been thinking about it." Henry paused, and then continued. "There's a fluidness to his action that means a lot of speed. But I guess we knew that."

"Yes, we did," Alec said quietly.

"He's short on stamina. His coat wasn't just wet. It was sweaty. He could use a lot of long, slow work. Not much time for that before the Hambletonian."

Alec said, "Get to the *real* problem, Henry. What about his wearing an open bridle?"

"It won't work, not now . . . not until he gets his self-confidence back."

"I thought you'd say that. Then what do we do? Try the blind again?"

Henry turned quickly to Alec. His surprise that Alec had even suggested the blind was evident in his eyes. He didn't answer right away. He was too pleased. Finally he said, "I don't know, Alec. I doubt that it would work any better than when Tom tried it."

Alec didn't say anything so Henry continued, "From what you told me, Bonfire jumped when the partial blind allowed him to see your horse a little ahead of him. Of course the colt had known you were on his right all the time, but he only got scared an' bolted when he saw how close you were."

"It would be that way in a race," Alec pointed out.

"I know," Henry replied thoughtfully. After a few seconds he asked, "What do you think about using a closed blind on him?"

Alec shook his head. "I don't think he'd stand for not being able to see anything with his right eye."

"But do you think it would work?" Henry asked persistently.

"Yes, if he'd wear it," Alec admitted. "Another horse would be well past before he'd be able to see him with just his left eye. I don't think he'd be scared then."

"And if he's not scared he won't jump," Henry said.

"That's right. But I'm sure he won't take the closed blind, Henry. He'll fight it."

"Let's find out this afternoon," Henry suggested. "We got to start someplace. It might as well be with that."

As matters turned out, it wasn't necessary to take Bonfire to the track to learn his reaction to the closed blind. They found out everything they needed to know right in the stable area.

They led him from his stall and put on the bridle with a blind that completely shut off all vision from his right eye. For a few seconds he stood still as though waiting patiently for them to remove the obstruction to his sight. When they didn't, a mounting restlessness swept over his red body. He shook his head to rid himself of the blind. When that did no good he rose high in the air, pawing in his fury.

They got him down, and removed the blind. After a long rest they tried again. It was no different this time. Once more he waited for them to relieve him of the darkness to his right. He was patient, tolerating the obstruction for a few seconds. Then his uneasiness mounted. He showed it first in a slight trembling of his red body. Then he rose on his hind legs as before, pawing the air, and throwing himself to the side.

They got out of his way, holding him with the long lead rope. He rose again, fighting more furiously than ever.

"It's no use, Henry," Alec said. "He'll never stand for it."

"Not long enough to run a race with it," Henry agreed, disappointed.

They got Bonfire down and, after removing the bridle, put him in his stall. Henry went to the tack trunk and sat down while Alec remained at the half-door, watching the colt.

"He'll tolerate the blind for about ten seconds," Alec said, "but no longer."

"About that, I guess," Henry admitted. "An' ten seconds aren't goin' to do us any good." He swung his feet together, his bowlegs almost forming a circle. "Well, we're back where we started. My first suggestion didn't amount to much."

For a few minutes neither spoke. Alec watched Bonfire pulling at the hay from the corner rack. "It'd be all right if we could turn the blind on and off," he said.

"Open and shut, y'mean," Henry corrected casually. And then he turned quickly to Alec, but the boy's back was toward him. "Open and shut?" he repeated, and the lightness had left his voice.

Alec shrugged his shoulders. "Well, you know what I mean, Henry. Open when we don't need it, closed when we do—and for no more than ten seconds." He laughed. "A silly idea. I wonder whatever made me think of a thing like that?" he added thoughtfully.

"Alec . . ." Henry began. But he didn't get a chance to finish, for Alec had turned toward him, his eyes bright and searching.

"Henry, didn't you once tell me about . . ."

"Halcyon?" Henry asked.

Alec nodded. "Then you're thinking about the same thing I am," he said.

"If it's Halcyon, it is," Henry answered. "He was the only running horse I know to wear that kind of a blinker hood.

Years ago it was, on a New York track."

"Didn't you tell me that the eyecups on that special hood could be opened and closed just by the jockey pulling a cord he held in his hands along with the reins?" Alec asked.

Henry nodded. "As I remember, the eyecups were controlled by small springs. So they worked like a shutter or a Venetian blind. The jock could open and close them as he saw fit during a race."

"Couldn't we do the same thing?" Alec asked eagerly. "Use a hood on Bonfire with just the right eyecup, and have the cord come back along the lines to me? Couldn't we, Henry?"

"We could if I can get to New York and find the right man to make such a hood for me."

"What's stopping you?"

"Nothing," Henry said, getting off the tack trunk. "I'm practically there now!"

Alec watched Henry go toward the parking area where his car was parked. It was a long chance they were taking, but a good one.

Follow the Leader

7

Henry didn't return that night or early the next morning. Alec took care of Bonfire but postponed eating breakfast, hoping that Henry would arrive and join him. By nine o'clock there still was no sign of Henry, so Alec ate alone.

Returning to the stables, he took Bonfire out for a walk, and then let him graze. The colt wore a light sheet, for the sky was a dull gray and there was dampness in the air. Horses and drivers went by on their way to the training track but they held no interest for Alec. He thought only of Henry. Had he found a man in New York who could make the special hood? Henry knew his way around. He'd spent half his life in New York. But even if his trip were successful would the trick hood work on Bonfire?

A large horse van passed. Alec watched it come to a stop before the nearest green-and-yellow sheds. The side door was lowered and heavy fiber matting laid over it so the horses to be loaded wouldn't slip. It wasn't difficult for Alec to identify the horses and know where they were going.

They were all three-year-olds bound for Goshen, New York, and the Hambletonian. Silver Knight was there, his large gray head held firmly by his groom. *If it hadn't been for him,* Alec thought, *things wouldn't be as bad as they are for Bonfire or Tom.* Yet how could he blame Silver Knight? It was the breaks of the game.

Eight other horses followed the gray colt into the van, their legs carefully bandaged, their bodies blanketed. Alec recognized Lively Man, who'd won the race that first night, and several others, including Victory Boy, who'd finished second. It was a valuable cargo the van was carrying. Every colt in it would soon race for a purse of well over a hundred thousand dollars.

The trainer-drivers supervised the loading of their colts. They were young men for the most part, men who were physically able to stand the strenuous demands of long days and still longer nights at Roosevelt Raceway. Alec could well understand why older men like George and Jimmy Creech preferred to race at the fairs. He turned toward Bonfire.

"Mister," he told the colt, "you'll be going to Goshen yourself pretty soon now." But he didn't feel as confident as his words implied. He kept wishing Henry would get back.

It was more than an hour later when Henry's car pulled into the stable area. Bonfire was back in his stall, so Alec hurried to meet his friend.

Henry got out of the car, his eyes tired and his unshaven face bristling with gray hairs. His hands were empty.

"Didn't you get it?" Alec asked quickly.

"You think I would have stayed up all night for nothin'?" Henry growled. "Sure I got it." He reached into the back of his black coupe and tossed the hood to Alec. "I had him make it red," he said, "figuring we'd better stick to Jimmy's stable colors."

As they walked back to their shed, Alec fingered the light racing hood with its bulging leather eyecup that opened and closed when he worked a spring catch.

Henry said, "All we got to do now is to attach a long cord to the catch an' we're ready to go."

"Plenty of cord around," Alec answered.

"Let's get to it, then."

"You mean you want to take him out now? . . . Today?"

"Why not?" Henry asked.

"Don't you think we should give him a day's rest? He hasn't had much since his fall."

"He's had plenty, Alec. An' the sooner we find out if this thing's goin' to work, the better off we'll be." They came to a stop before Bonfire's stall, and Alec let the colt sniff the red hood.

Henry went on, "Besides, this colt could be jogged every day for the next few months without it hurtin' him any. That's what he needs. He's long on speed, but short on stamina for a race like the Hambletonian."

Taking the hood from Alec, Henry went into the stall. "I want to get this over with so I can get some sleep," he grumbled.

"Then you think it's going to work?"

"It's not goin' to take long to find out," Henry answered, slipping the hood over Bonfire's head.

The colt didn't object, for the eyecup was open, and the light hood was easy and comfortable to wear. "Now get the bridle and the harness," Henry requested.

A few minutes later they took Bonfire from his stall. "I don't think we should hitch him to the cart right away," Alec commented. "If it doesn't work and he goes up he might hurt himself on the shafts."

"You're right," Henry agreed. "Now get the cord, Alec."

The cord was attached to the spring catch and then taken back along the right line, passing through the harness terret to Alec. He was careful with the cord, knowing that the slightest pull would close the eyecup. He tied it around his little finger to keep it separate from the lines.

"Okay, Henry," Alec called. "I'm ready when you are."

Henry led Bonfire down the shed row. Finally he called, "Close it, Alec!" He watched the colt. Bonfire kept walking quietly beside him. "Open it!" No more than a couple of seconds had passed with the cup closed.

"How'd it go?" Alec asked from behind the colt.

"Fine," Henry answered. "We'll keep this up for a little while, gradually lengthening the time the cup's closed. This is goin' to work, Alec!"

For more than thirty minutes they walked Bonfire up and down the shed row, opening and closing the eyecup. Toward the end they kept it closed for many seconds, but never long enough so that the colt was ready to fight the blind. They found that his uneasiness left him quickly once they opened the cup and that they could close it again after a short interval.

Finally they hitched Bonfire and took him to the track. They said nothing on the way there, each knowing how optimistic the other felt but realizing that the final test would come on the track.

Henry left Bonfire's side when they reached the gate.

"Okay, Alec," he said, "you two are on your own now."

Alec took the colt up the homestretch, conscious of glances from the men sitting on the benches. But they weren't overcurious. Racing hoods weren't unusual. Only if the men happened to see the eyecup close would their interest be aroused.

Alec kept Bonfire near the outside rail, and found no need to close the cup. Other horses went by but they were all far enough away not to bother Bonfire. When they passed Henry for the first time, Alec saw him signal to move the colt over.

Alec obeyed, looking behind as he did so. Several horses were coming up on his right. He waited until they were close beside him and then pulled the cord. It took only a second or two for the horses to pass and get well in front of Bonfire. Alec opened the eyecup again, and Bonfire never broke stride when he saw the horses ahead of him. Instead, his eagerness to catch up with them was disclosed in the sudden pricking up of his ears. He asked for more line and Alec gave it to him.

The colt picked up more speed quickly. He was eager to go on as he swept past the horses, but Alec slowed him down again.

He kept Bonfire a few lengths ahead of the other horses going around the turn and into the backstretch. He'd found out the trick hood was successful and, furthermore, that there was no need to close the eyecup when Bonfire *passed* horses to his right. It was only when they came up on him that he was reminded of his clash with Silver Knight.

Alec slowed Bonfire still more, letting the horses come up on his right again. Once more he closed the eyecup when they passed, and then opened it. When Bonfire saw the horses ahead of him he wanted to go after them as he had done before, but Alec kept him behind. The boy wanted to shout to Henry that the hood was working better than his most hopeful expectations. But when they passed the old trainer, all Alec did was to nod his head. And Henry nodded back.

Henry watched them go up the stretch, the colt striding so easily and Alec sitting so relaxed behind him. The trick hood was working all right, working for both of them. Henry couldn't recall ever having felt much better than he did just then. He wasn't even tired after his long night.

Later, back at the stables, Henry said, "I think I'll let you go in a race with him in a few nights."

"So soon, Henry?" Alec asked anxiously. "Do you think he'll be ready for it?"

"He has to be, if we're goin' to Goshen. It's not 'so soon,' Alec. We got less than two weeks now to the Hambletonian."

Alec remembered the colts he'd seen being sent to Goshen that morning and nodded. "You're right, Henry. He ought to get a good race in him."

"I guess so," the old trainer replied. And he hoped desperately that he was right.

They entered Bonfire in a race for Monday night, three days off. The blood bay colt went to the track on Saturday and Sunday, with Henry watching his every move—and Alec's too. Everything he saw was most encouraging but he knew he was rushing them a little in having them go to the post Monday night. Yet he had no alternative. The Hambletonian would take place a week from the following Wednesday, and the colt definitely needed the race on Monday. So did Alec.

Henry was gambling that everything would go well for them. If it did there'd be no holding them down. They'd both have the confidence they needed, thanks to the trick hood. If things didn't go well and they got in a jam, well . . . As he thought of the consequences, Henry covered his face with the palms of his big hands.

Then his hopes rose again when he remembered how docile Bonfire was while wearing the hood and that Alec had no trouble working the eyecup. It seemed to Henry that working it came automatically to Alec now. The boy knew to the exact second when to close and when to open it.

On Sunday morning Alec finished the long four-mile jog Henry had ordered for Bonfire. He was about to take the colt off the track when Henry said, "Don't go back yet, Alec. I want you to turn him an' go a fast quarter just to top him off for tomorrow night."

As Alec took Bonfire up the track, ready and anxious to go, the colt too knew what was coming. Except for the Black, Alec had never felt more alertness and eagerness in any horse than he did during the seconds he stopped Bonfire at the head of the stretch and then turned him the right way of the track. He thought the blood bay colt was going to break from his hands. The colt demanded rather than requested more rein. Alec had to use all his skill in keeping down Bonfire's strides until they'd reached the starting pole, and then he let him go.

Bonfire's speed was not gradual, mounting, when Alec gave him his long awaited release. It came with a sudden burst of swiftness that caught Alec unprepared. He felt the seat beneath him move as though it were alive. He was picked up and hurled forward with it, and all the terrific pull of Bonfire ran down the lines to his arms and shoulders. He pushed his feet hard against the stirrup irons to keep from being lifted bodily from his seat.

Had he ever thought there was *little* difference between driving and riding a racehorse? If so, he quickly changed his mind as the white rail whipped by in a never-ending blur. Riding was being a part of your horse, being one with him, going along with him stride for stride. This was something else. This was being whipped along in the wake of a flaming meteor. He sat so low, so close to Bonfire's powerful hind-quarters, that he had to lean to the left in order to see what was ahead. The track was clear. They were going around the sharp first turn, yet there was no slackening of Bonfire's long strides. Alec kept him close to the rail.

Off the turn and down the backstretch they went, the colt's long tail lashing his rider's face. Alec leaned farther to the left to avoid the tail and to watch for the quarter-mile pole. He saw that they were rapidly approaching the pole. He called to Bonfire, urging him on to still greater speed. The black tail streamed back, whipping harder. Alec felt its sting, but didn't mind now. Tomorrow night he'd sit on it. *Tail-sitter!* He called to his colt again and they flashed by the quarter-mile pole.

A few minutes later he drove Bonfire back to the stables. Henry walked alongside. "You seemed to have a little trouble slowin' him down after the quarter pole," the old trainer said.

"It wasn't as easy as I'd thought it'd be," Alec answered. "He wanted to go on."

"Nothin' wrong with his feelin' that way. It was a good show. Even the guys sittin' on the bench with me were impressed."

"Weren't you, Henry?"

"Yeah, but I figured he had that kind of speed."

Alec said, "It was an experience I won't forget very soon. It was different from riding fast, and I hadn't figured on that, somehow. It felt, well, like . . ." He stopped, and then went on, "It's hard to explain, Henry. But don't you feel that this sport is growing on you too?"

"No, but the colt is," Henry answered quietly.

The next day, race day, they did nothing but walk Bonfire, and then waited for the night to come.

It was late in the afternoon that the waiting became most difficult. Bonfire was going to the post in the first race of the evening at eight-thirty. And now, at not quite six o'clock, they watched the horses Bonfire would be racing against go to the track for their first mile warm-up.

To get away from seeing them, Alec went to the tack room. Waiting was hard enough without having to watch their competition at this early hour. These horses would give Bonfire the kind of race he needed. The colt should win if everything went well. The horses Alec was really worried about beating were at Goshen, awaiting the Hambletonian.

Momentarily he let his thoughts turn to Tom. The operation was over and, according to the post card received from George the day before, it had been a complete success. Tom would be in the hospital a week more, and then would be allowed to go home on crutches. Jimmy Creech, who had met George and Tom at the Pittsburgh airport, was with them.

Alec left the tack room. Thinking of Tom hadn't helped him to forget tonight's race. He passed Henry and went into the stall with Bonfire. This was the best place for him just now.

The blood bay colt left the corner of his stall, and went to Alec. He stood quietly beside the boy without nickering, without nuzzling.

Alec pulled the red-and-white cooler a little higher on Bonfire's neck, but after that left him alone. It was enough just to be with him. He was certain the colt felt the same way about his being there.

"You need a mascot, somebody like Napoleon," he told him after a while. "You don't like to be left alone, do you?"

Bonfire turned his head toward him but made no sound. Alec went on talking softly to him.

A few minutes later the door opened and Henry came inside. He stood quietly beside Alec a little while and then said, "They just came back."

"Who?" Alec asked without taking his eyes off Bonfire.

"The horses we'll be racing against," Henry answered. He shook his white head, puzzled. "The things they do here, an' nobody tells me why."

Alec said nothing but his friend went on anyway. "I got to talkin' to some of the young fellows yesterday while watchin' you and Bonfire. One of them was Fred Ringo, who has that Hambletonian colt Lively Man up at Goshen. He flies up there just to work his colt, an' then comes back here to train and race his other horses."

"He's got a big stable," Alec pointed out.

"I know. So have a good many of the other young trainers here, an' they all seem to be makin' big money." Henry paused. "But that's not what I had in mind to tell you about."

Alec kept his eyes on Bonfire, talking to the colt by glances and touches alone.

Henry continued, "I asked them why they thought they had to give their horses as much as *three* separate mile warm-ups before going to the post. You think I got an answer, Alec?"

Alec shrugged his shoulders. "I don't know, Henry," he said. He well remembered finding Bonfire standing hot and blowing in his paddock stall upon his arrival at Roosevelt Raceway. It wouldn't be that way tonight. Henry had ordered no pre-race works for Bonfire.

"Well, I got no answer," Henry went on. "Most of the men just looked at me like I shouldn't even have asked. An' this Fred Ringo said, *'It's the way it's done.'* I got up an' left 'em." Henry paused before continuing. "What I should have told them, Alec, is that that was the way it was done when I was their age, but there's no sane reason for doin' it *now*. I should've told them to look at their horses instead of at me!"

Alec turned to Henry, and noticed that his face was getting red. "Don't get excited, Henry. You'll bother the colt."

"I'm not excited," the old trainer said, lowering his voice. "It just makes me sore to see what these young guys, who call themselves *trainers* as well as drivers, are doin'. They're not even thinkin' for themselves. They're following the leader . . . the *old* leaders! It was the way we did it many years ago, when we unhitched horses from wagons and plows in the fields an' then took them to the track for a day of racing."

Henry bent down to check Bonfire's leg bandages but it

didn't stop him from talking. Alec listened. He had learned long ago to listen to everything Henry had to say.

"Of course *our* horses needed those long, hard warm-ups just before their races," Henry was saying. "They were rugged, strong animals doin' the work that tractors do today, an' knowin' little else except an occasional day off to race at a fair. They were muscle-bound. We worked them before the race to loosen 'em up because we knew they'd race all the better for it."

Henry shook his head sadly. "But that stuff isn't necessary today. If the guys around here would look at their horses they'd know it. These horses have come a long way since I was a kid. They're not bred and raised to work a field any more, but for *speed*. Years and years of fine, close line breeding have made them what they are today, lighter boned, lighter bodied, more temperamental, and much faster than anything we ever dreamed of when I was a kid. Most of 'em don't need the kind of hard work they're gettin' before goin' to the post. They're leavin' their races on the warm-up track."

Henry went to Bonfire and pulled the colt's forelock away from his eyes. "Some of 'em are takin' all that work better'n others. But one thing I know for sure is that *this* colt can't take it. Thanks to the Black he's as racy as anything I've ever seen at our tracks. He's got the Black's hot blood. He'll know when he's about to race. His coat will get wet without any work before goin' to the post. He'll loosen himself up without any help from us. A light jog on the way to the post is all he needs . . . an' it's all he'll get while I'm trainin' him."

Then Henry turned to Alec, grinning a little self-consciously. "That was a long spiel," he said. "You're a good listener, an' plenty patient."

Alec put a hand on Henry's arm. "What do you think I'm here for? I want to listen to you and learn as much as I can."

Henry chuckled. "I thought it was jus' because you liked my company, Alec."

"It's that too," Alec answered.

Henry turned back to Bonfire. "Anyway," he said, "for him an' for us there's not goin' to be any 'follow the leader' stuff . . . those old leaders like Jimmy Creech who never change their way of doin' things."

Suddenly they heard a high nasal voice call, "Henry! Henry Dailey! Are you in this row?"

Henry's face went white and he stood frozen in his position beside Bonfire. Alec went to the stall door and saw a skinny little man with a prominent nose walking toward them. He stopped when he came to the stall with Bonfire's nameplate above the door, and then he looked in.

Alec couldn't take his eyes off this strange, scrawny-looking little man. He heard Henry say in a tight voice, "Hello, Jimmy."

The Leader

8

So this was Jimmy Creech. Alec watched him walk into the stall unmindful of anything or anybody but *his* colt. Bonfire went to him, pushing his nose into Jimmy's thin chest. Jimmy stroked him, and in his small eyes was the devoted, loving look of a father for his only son. It said, "This is *my* colt."

Alec turned to Henry, who was strangely quiet for one who had just met an old friend. But so was Jimmy Creech. Alec turned back to him and the colt.

Finally Jimmy said, without taking his eyes off Bonfire, "I had to come and see how you were making out with him. Tom told me to come. He said it would do me good, and he was right."

"You don't look so well, Jimmy," Henry said. "Are you sure you're feelin' okay?"

"I'm fine now," Jimmy answered.

"Did you tell your doctor you were comin'?"

"No. He wouldn't have let me come, if I had. He's got me down for just one visit to the track this year. I picked the

83

Hambletonian." For the first time Jimmy turned to Henry. "Will he be goin' in it, Henry?"

"I think so."

Jimmy turned back to Bonfire. "That's what I wanted to hear you say. That's why I came. Just to hear that and look at him again. It's been a long time, over two months now. No doctor should mind my having so little as this, and then going right home."

Henry's face lightened. "What time does your train leave, Jim?" he asked.

"Ten o'clock. A sleeper to Pittsburgh, so I'll get plenty of rest." Jimmy looked at Alec. "Tom and George told me about you," he said kindly. "A lot of good things, too." He let his sick eyes fasten themselves on Bonfire again. "Do you like him?"

"They don't come any better," Alec answered.

Jimmy's scrawny shoulders came back a little in his pride, and he nodded his head in full agreement with Alec. "Tell me what you've done for him, Henry," he requested.

Henry shifted uneasily. "He's going well. We're usin' a blind on him, Jim."

Alec saw the tightness come to Jimmy's face as the little man said in a quivering voice, "I like my colts to go clean. You know that."

"I do too," Henry came back quietly. "But sometimes it's necessary to use an aid. We had to here."

Alec noted the mounting anger in Jimmy's face and said quickly, "It's really a wonderful idea, sir. He wears a hood and we can open and close the eyecup. Look, let me show it to you." He left the stall without seeing the warning in Henry's eyes.

When Jimmy took the racing hood from Alec, his face was livid. Alec saw the look in Henry's eyes then, and realized he had done wrong in producing the hood for Jimmy's examination.

For a moment Jimmy just held the hood in his trembling hands, looking at it, but saying nothing. His body was shaking too.

Henry came up behind him, speaking softly. He told him what they had done and why. He explained how well the special hood was working and that it would get their colt to the Hambletonian. Wasn't that what Jimmy wanted more than anything else in the world? After the big race the hood could be removed from Bonfire. The colt was regaining his self-confidence quickly. He wouldn't need the hood much longer. It was just a temporary aid. But it was necessary now if they were to race Bonfire. Couldn't Jimmy look at it that way?

Alec knew that Jimmy was doing everything he could to understand and to accept the hood as a temporary aid for Bonfire. His fight to keep from becoming overexcited was evident in his eyes and pitiful to see. Alec understood then why Jimmy's doctor didn't want him to visit the track.

There was silence in the stall long after Henry had finished talking. Even Bonfire was quiet. Finally Jimmy handed back the hood to Alec. "All right, Henry," he said softly, steadily. "I see why you had to use it."

Nothing more was said for a while. Jimmy walked slowly around Bonfire, feeling the colt's legs and body, lifting and examining his feet. When he had finished, he said reluctantly, "I guess that's what I came for. Maybe it would be best if I went now."

Henry said, "I'll drive you to Mineola. It's only an hour's ride from there to New York."

"I know," Jimmy replied. "That's the way I came. But you needn't bother, Henry. I'll get a taxi."

Henry chuckled easily. "Bother? For an old friend? What are you talkin' about, Jimmy? It'll give us a little more time together. Come on. Alec will take care of the colt. There's nothin' to keep me here."

Jimmy took a long last look at Bonfire and then left the stall. As Alec watched him go, he felt he understood now why Tom had wanted to do so much for Jimmy Creech. There were few such men left, old-timers who had devoted all their lives to their horses and loved them beyond everything else. In addition, Jimmy was a very sick man.

Alec saw him come to a sudden stop outside the stall, and then Jimmy asked Henry in his high voice, "When you going to start him? He'll need a race before going to Goshen."

There it was. Alec felt a numbness sweep over him. Henry wouldn't lie to Jimmy. It wasn't in him to lie about anything.

"Soon," Henry told Jimmy quietly. "Come on, now. We'd better get goin'. We'll have more time together at the station."

But Jimmy wasn't to be put off. "It's got to be this week. Didn't you put your entry in the box yet?"

Henry nodded his big head.

"Well, when is he going then?"

Henry stopped, and his tortured gaze met Jimmy's. "Tonight," he said.

"Tonight?"

Henry nodded again.

"What race?" Jimmy asked, and there was mounting excitement in his voice, his eyes, in everything about him.

Alec waited for Henry's reply, and finally it came. "The first race."

There was no holding Jimmy now. "I can see it then," he said eagerly. "I can sneak it in without my doctor knowing. It'll still leave me time to catch my train from New York, won't it, Henry?"

"I guess so," Henry returned grudgingly, "but don't you think it might be wiser if—"

"You talk like my doctor," Jimmy interrupted, irritation creeping into his voice. "I can just see *you* going home under the same circumstances!" He looked back at the stall and then at Henry again.

"If he's going in the first race, why aren't you warming him up?" Jimmy glanced at his wrist watch. "He should have made a trip by this time."

"He's not going," Henry said in a low voice. "He doesn't need any before his race."

"He doesn't *what?*"

"He doesn't need any trips," Henry repeated. Then he added, "Now take it easy, Jim, an' let me explain why. I know you've always warmed up your horses, same as you did when we were kids. But this colt don't need that kind of pre-race work. It knocks him out. He's a speed colt. He's not built or bred for all that work before a race. It tires him out. He'll leave his race on the warm-up track."

Jimmy made no effort to control himself as he'd done when confronted with the special hood. His voice was shrill as he answered Henry. "*You're* telling *me* about *my* colt!"

Again Henry said, "Now take it easy, Jim. Please. I was just tryin' to explain how—"

Jimmy interrupted, "—how to train my colt, that's what you were trying to do! *You,* who wouldn't have anything to do with my kind of horses!" Jimmy's face was white with rage.

Henry said as quietly as he could, "That was years ago. I don't feel that way now, Jim. I'm tryin' to help." He paused. "I got a right to tell you what I think about this colt. An' I don't think race day is the time to train him."

"You got no right to tell me anything if you don't train him the way it's supposed to be done!" Jimmy bellowed.

"If I don't train him the way *it's supposed to be done,*" Henry repeated slowly.

Alec saw the tiny pinpoints of light come to Henry's eyes. *Please, Henry, keep quiet,* he thought. *Let Jimmy do the talking. Remember he's a sick man. You get mad at what he's saying, and you won't do the colt or us any good.*

But Alec's pleading thoughts were of no help, for Henry said bitterly, "Why don't you look at your colt, Jimmy? You can see what I see if you'll just let yourself be reasonable. It's not hard. He's not like the others you've had. He doesn't have to be trained the way *it's supposed to be done* at all."

"Stop it!" Jimmy's voice shrilled up and down the shed row. Grooms in nearby stalls stopped their work to turn and look at him.

It was many seconds before Jimmy had control of himself, and then his words came pouring out while his pointed Adam's apple rose high in his thin neck. "I've taken all I can from you, Henry! You tell me to look at my colt. You tell me how to train him. *You,* who never even sat behind a fast horse. You're telling *me*. Get out of here. Get out quick before I throw you out!"

He turned to Alec. "You go with him! I don't need *you,* either!"

The blood rushed to Alec's head. He turned toward Henry, but his old friend wasn't looking at him. Instead Henry was walking down the row, his bowlegs moving like a very slow wheel, his big shoulders stooped and beaten.

Tears came to Alec's eyes. He could hardly see Jimmy standing there in front of him. He heard Bonfire moving about to his rear, and then felt the colt's warm breath on the back of his neck. He heard himself say, "I want to stay. I've got to stay."

Jimmy shouted, "Then you do it my way!" He whirled to watch Henry, who was far down the row.

After many minutes Jimmy turned back to Alec. He was no longer furious but terribly weary. Yet his jaw was set with pure mulishness, and Alec knew there'd be no backing down. He awaited Jimmy's orders. Finally they came.

"Let's hook him up," Jimmy said. "I want you to jog him a couple of miles. After that we'll turn him and go a mile in about two minutes ten seconds. No slower. You got a watch?"

"Yes, sir."

Jimmy looked at Alec and then said more kindly, "Henry's all wrong, you know. With our horses y'got to get them really loosened up before they race. It not only helps their muscles but it gets them to a high racing pitch. They're ready to go then. Any temperament has been taken out of them. They don't do any jumping around. They keep their minds on the business at hand."

Alec listened, realizing that Jimmy believed everything he said. No one was going to argue him into believing that Bonfire didn't need to follow this set training routine. And Alec didn't find this so strange when he thought of the younger men at Roosevelt Raceway. They did things no differently. They followed the leader, as Henry had said, and here was one of the leaders—Jimmy.

He put the hood on Bonfire while Jimmy got the bridle and harness. As they worked, Alec got up courage to say, "You're sure you want me to go that fast a mile with him on the training track?"

"Sure I do," Jimmy said stubbornly. "He'll be going faster than that before you're through warming him up. I want the second and third mile trips to be down around two minutes five or six seconds."

Alec said, "That's almost fast enough to win a Hambletonian."

"That's what we're aimin' to do next week," Jimmy answered.

Alec stayed behind as Jimmy led Bonfire from the stall. With all this scheduled work it was going to be really rough out there tonight. He wondered if Henry would be around to watch the race.

By seven-thirty they had Bonfire in the paddock. Two of the three separate mile warm-ups were behind the blood bay colt. And now, less than an hour before being called to the post, Alec drove him out on the main track for his last warm-up mile.

Alec was as hot as his colt from all the work they'd done in so short a time. He thought he'd never in his life forget Bonfire's second mile. The colt really had had to step along to finish it in the time Jimmy had ordered. This final trip was to be as fast. Under any other circumstances Alec would have been overjoyed at the prospect of another fast ride behind Bonfire. As it was, he couldn't be very happy knowing there was still a race to be run.

It wasn't yet dark but the track lights were on, and the great stands were beginning to fill. There were many horses on the track, all working, and Alec paid attention to them only because of Bonfire's eyecup. He had to be ready to close it any time a horse came up close on their right.

Bonfire tossed his head a little. He was wearing the number 5 on his head now that they were on the main track. It was a raceway rule, just as it was a rule that the drivers be wearing their racing silks at this time. Alec glanced at the sleeves of his red-and-white jacket—Tom's jacket and Jimmy's colors.

Bonfire was eager to go again, for his red coat was very wet; too wet, Henry would have said. Alec looked over at the stands, wondering if Henry was there.

He knew Henry was right about Bonfire. Already the colt had done too much work. Through the lines Alec felt a lack of the sharpness that had been in Bonfire during the last mile.

He turned the colt at the top of the stretch and took him down, giving him full line as they swept past the starting pole. At the same time he pushed down the stem of his watch, starting the sweeping second hand. Henry had always said that he didn't need to carry a watch, that he had one in his head. But Alec didn't want to take any chances at guessing Bonfire's pace just now, with Jimmy demanding another 2:06 mile on the dot: "No slower, no faster."

Alec felt the sulky seat leap from under him as he asked Bonfire for speed. It seemed more alive than it had the first day he had worked Bonfire for Henry. The seat of the racing sulky was much closer to the colt's hindquarters than that of the training cart, and Alec felt as though he were being carried along on Bonfire's flying heels. He sat on the colt's tail, leaned a little to the side so he could see the track, and went on.

Around the half-mile oval they raced and whipped past the stands again, going into the second lap. Alec glanced at his watch and kept Bonfire down to the same speed. When they had gone three-quarters of a mile he looked at the watch once more, and then let the colt out another notch.

Bonfire quickly responded and came flying off the back turn into the homestretch. All the way down to the finish line he demanded more rein from Alec. But Alec held him in, completing the mile in the time Jimmy had ordered.

A little later he drove Bonfire through the paddock gate. Jimmy took the colt's bridle, saying, "Nice going, Alec. Now we're all set to race."

Alec wondered. He'd know for certain in about forty minutes, when they went to the post. He'd know the second they stepped onto the track again and he felt Bonfire through the lines.

The Old Hand

9

The paddock bell sounded and the gate to the track was opened. Over the public-address system came the bugle call to the post, and then the announcer said, "Ladies and gentlemen, the horses are now coming onto the track for the first race of the evening's program."

Jimmy Creech removed the worn white cooler with the badly faded red borders from Bonfire's back. He stepped away. "Good luck, Alec." He watched Bonfire pass through the gate, the fifth horse in the field of eight.

Jimmy carefully folded the blanket, and then pressed it lovingly against his scrawny chest. Everything else for Bonfire was newly bought and slick and polished—the black harness, the red hood, and the sulky with its glistening wheels. But the old blanket held many fond memories, and tonight, as in races long since past, it would bring luck to his horse, even though he wasn't up behind this colt, the finest of them all!

He turned to watch the marshal who rode the colorful palomino horse at the head of the post parade. He noted with scorn the man's white form-fitting coat and pants, his shiny black boots and peaked hunting cap. All so dashing beneath this galaxy of lights, all so sickening compared to the county fairs Jimmy had known and loved.

Jimmy looked for Bonfire when he heard the announcer begin to introduce the horses. There was a bench just inside the track where he could sit if he liked. But he didn't want to sit there tonight. He felt the hot surging of his blood, the increased beat of his heart.

"Don't get panicky now," he told himself. "There's plenty of time. Plenty."

He left the security and comparative privacy of the paddock for the swarming crowd standing on the cement apron before the great stands. He pushed his way through the people. He wanted to get near the center of the stretch where he'd be able to see his colt start and finish. He carried the worn blanket beneath his arm.

His heart beat faster as he came nearer to where he wanted to be, and despite the rumbling, loud cries of the milling crowd, his ears heard only the voice of the announcer. He listened eagerly for what he wanted to hear, and at last it came.

"Number five is Bonfire, a blood bay colt sired by the Black and out of Volo Queen. Bonfire is owned by Mr. Jimmy Creech of Coronet, Pennsylvania and is being driven by Alec Ramsay."

Jimmy listened and sought to still the pounding of his heart. Owned by Jimmy Creech. Bred by Jimmy Creech. Raised by Jimmy Creech. Broken by Jimmy Creech. Trained by Jimmy Creech. After sixty-three years of waiting, waiting for this *one*.

"This is my colt," he wanted to shout to those around him. "This is the result of all I've worked for. Look upon him. He carries the blood of the finest mare I ever bred and raced. No, not a great mare. She saved her greatness for her colt, this colt in whose blood along with hers is that of a fine stallion. A great stallion but one never before bred to a harness mare; therefore untried and unsought by the rest of you who seek change only by turning night into day with your bright lights and fancy frills! You seek perfection in the extravaganza of your colored stages such as this. I seek it in a horse. And there he is. Look upon him, all of you!"

The marshal left the horses at the head of the stretch, and they came down in their first warm-up score. Jimmy watched Bonfire's every stride, reveling in the beauty of the colt's long legs. He was most proud, and confident of victory for his colt. Didn't every person there see all that he did?

He glanced self-consciously at the people standing near him. Their eyes weren't on Bonfire as he went by. They were watching a tall chestnut horse warming up close to the rail.

"That's Streamliner," he heard a woman say excitedly.

Jimmy's puzzled gaze remained on her. Was she so impressed by the fact that six years before Streamliner had placed third in the Hambletonian? Was she unable to see any other horse on the track, including his colt? Didn't she know that she was looking at an aged horse, one who should have been retired long ago? Wouldn't she rather look at a colt who was young and on his way to greatness?

Jimmy turned away from her in search of other people who did appreciate the grace, the smoothness of Bonfire as he went by again. Only then did he see, a short distance away, the man whose head followed the movement of the blood bay colt all the way down the stretch. But Jimmy quickly turned away, for the man was Henry.

A few minutes later the horses reached the mobile starting gate and followed it around the back turn. Suddenly Jimmy felt nausea sweep over him. He took the folded blanket from beneath his arm and pressed it close to his stomach, hoping its warmth would keep him from vomiting. He mustn't get sick now. He must see the race tonight, and next week the Hambletonian. Then he would be content to do as his doctor had recommended and never watch another race.

The gate was moving faster. The horses followed it past the stands. Jimmy watched Bonfire. Alec had him a few strides behind the horse on his right. The eyecup was open. But nearing the starting line Alec began moving up. The eyecup closed as Bonfire raced alongside the number six horse in close quarters behind the barrier.

Jimmy pressed the blanket harder against his stomach, and the beat of his heart seemed to pound louder than all the horses' hoofs. *If it was like this for him tonight, how would he ever be able to watch his colt in the Hambletonian?*

The car swept across the starting line, its long barrier wings folding quickly at its sides. The lights in the stands dimmed. The race was on!

In the first great surge Jimmy saw Bonfire's hooded head in front. He shouted at the top of his voice. He saw the eyecup open. He shouted again as Bonfire drew farther ahead going down to the turn. His speed was so great that Alec was safely able to move him over to the rail, taking the lead.

"Look!" Jimmy shouted to everyone about him. "Now you'll look at him!"

Over the public-address system the announcer said, "That's Bonfire out in front. Streamliner is second."

Jimmy found it hard to breathe. He opened his mouth, seeking more air. "You look too!" he wanted to tell Henry. "You didn't think he could do it!"

Going down the backstretch, Bonfire continued to pull away from the others. Was there ever a better striding colt? Was there ever one any faster? "No, no," Jimmy answered himself. "He's it. He's it."

"At the quarter-mile," the announcer called, "Bonfire has increased his lead to four lengths. Streamliner is second. Lady Luck is third. Worthy Lad is fourth . . ."

Jimmy glanced at the lights on the infield board that gave the time of the first quarter-mile. Satisfied, he turned back to watch the race. Alec had taken Bonfire to the quarter in just the time he'd ordered. Jimmy grinned. It was close to Hambletonian speed, and that's what he wanted from his colt tonight.

The horses came around the back turn, all in single file, taking the short mile by staying close to the rail. Bonfire raced alone, far ahead of the field. The people in the stands rose from their seats to acclaim this blood bay colt who was streaking down the homestretch for the first time.

Jimmy heard the ovation and his heart pounded harder than ever. He watched his colt approaching the stands. The eyecup was open. There'd be no need for Alec to close it again. No horse could catch up with Bonfire. But the special hood had made it possible for Bonfire to race tonight. Jimmy glanced kindly in Henry's direction. In his pride he could afford to be forgiving and appreciative.

Suddenly the ovation for Bonfire stopped. He was passing the stands but he didn't seem to be drawing ahead of the others. Jimmy glanced back at Streamliner. The chestnut horse was gaining on Bonfire! Or was Bonfire tiring? Jimmy's eyes were so blurred it was hard for him to tell.

Then the crowd began shouting again. But for Jimmy it was a different kind of clamoring. The spectators were now urging Streamliner on in his drive to catch Bonfire! It seemed to take the blood bay colt a long time to reach the half-mile pole, where the race had begun, and Jimmy found himself counting off the seconds.

The announcer called, "At the half-mile it's Bonfire still in front by half a length. Streamliner is second. Lady Luck is third. Worthy Lad . . ."

But Jimmy wasn't listening. He looked at the time for the half-mile. Only the clock was important now. He found that Bonfire had gone two seconds slower in the half than he'd ordered. Jimmy was furious with Alec for having disobeyed his instructions. But then he saw Alec's raised hands, hands that were asking Bonfire for more speed without getting any response.

A slight twist of concern appeared on Jimmy's face. He watched Streamliner draw alongside Bonfire. The colt's eye-cup was closed. When Streamliner went by, the cup was opened again.

"Nothing's wrong," Jimmy told himself heatedly. "He'll come on again. He'll catch that chestnut horse soon."

But Streamliner lengthened his lead going into the first turn, and behind Bonfire came the others, closer and closer.

Maybe he's just a little tired, Jimmy thought, frantic now. *But he'll win. I'm sure he will.*

Lady Luck passed Bonfire, and Jimmy saw the eyecup close and then open again. This was repeated when Worthy Lad went by.

Jimmy realized then that for him and his tired colt the race was over. Yet he didn't feel sick, as he had before. He was too numb to feel anything but pity for his colt and shame for what he'd done to him.

Tears came to his eyes, and he didn't fight them back. He was glad they made it more difficult for him to see Bonfire dropping to the rear, with one horse after another passing him.

You told everyone else to look at him. Now you look at him. Look at him good. Look at him and remember all the things Henry told you a few hours ago. You did this to your colt.

Streamliner finished the race an easy winner in much slower time than Bonfire had worked his mile warm-ups for Jimmy.

The lights went on in the great stands and Jimmy started for the paddock. People pushed against him. He did not shove back, for both hands were clasping the folded, worn blanket. He let the crowd carry him forward. He felt many hands upon him but he didn't care. An arm went around his shoulders and he braced himself for the shove to come. But instead the arm guided him through the crowd. Then he turned to the man walking at his side.

"I've been a fool, Henry," he said, "—an old fool."

"No more than I, Jimmy," Henry answered quietly.

Goshen

10

Alec waited for Henry until long after midnight before going to bed. He lay in the darkness, wondering if Henry had gotten Jimmy safely on his train. Actually, Henry had driven his friend all the way to New York, for he'd been afraid to let him go alone. But Alec didn't know that. As he figured it, if everything had gone all right, Henry should have been back before now.

Alec listened for Bonfire but the colt was quiet. He'd cooled out well and showed no ill effects from his hard night's work except that he was tired.

The race had been a nightmare for Alec. It wasn't an easy thing to see a horse fighting to produce more speed, as Bonfire had done, with nothing left to give. That fast first quarter of a mile, which Jimmy had demanded of them, had taken all the colt could give after all his warm-ups. Alec knew that if only he had been allowed to rate Bonfire behind the others for most of the race he might have won. But it hadn't gone that way.

Alec turned on his other side. At least the race had accomplished something. Jimmy had seen for himself that Henry was right about the colt. No words could have done as much. After the race Jimmy had been a beaten man. He'd kept repeating that he was a fool, an old fool. And Henry kept saying that he was, too. It had been a strange aftermath to their previous fiery encounter.

An hour later Henry came into the tack room.

"Turn on the light," Alec said. "I'm awake."

"I can undress in the dark," Henry answered. "I've had enough lights for one night."

Alec wondered if he meant the track lights but didn't ask.

"Is Jimmy all right?"

"I guess so. I got him into his berth and waited until the train left. If he gets some sleep he should be okay by Pittsburgh."

Alec waited until Henry was in bed before speaking again. He wanted to talk about the race. He wanted Henry's assurance that everything was going to turn out all right for their colt. "If Jimmy had only listened to you, he would have had something good to take back with him. He'd have felt better instead of worse."

For many seconds Henry didn't answer and then he said, "I don't want to talk about it tonight, Alec. I'm as much to blame as he is for what happened. I lost my head when there were other ways to make him understand. I got him mad, and he took it out on you and Bonfire. He never would have made you go so fast in all those warm-ups otherwise."

Alec said, in justification of Henry, "You had to tell him how you felt about the colt."

"There were other ways of handling it," Henry replied.

"I've known Jimmy long enough to know what they were."

For a while Henry said nothing after that and Alec let him alone. Finally Henry said, more to himself than to Alec, "I remember when I was eighteen and Jimmy was twenty. He was drivin' his horses at the county fairs an' making money. I had nothing. No money, that is. I had a colt that could run. I rode him all the time. I wanted to become a jockey, not a driver.

"One day I knew I had my colt ready to race, but in order to do it I had to get him to a New York track. Jimmy loaned me the money to get us there and feed us for a couple of weeks. I knew that after that time my colt would be payin' our own way along. He did all right, and I paid Jimmy back. But I never went home."

Alec said, "Then if Jimmy hadn't loaned you that money you might not be what you are."

"That's right, Alec. Or here tonight, *feelin'* the way I do."

Nothing more was said and finally a restless sleep came to them.

In the morning Alec took Bonfire for a long walk to get rid of any stiffness in him, and then he let him graze. He watched his colt for any sign of lameness but Bonfire was sound and ready to go. Alec wondered how long they'd remain at Roosevelt Raceway. There was no reason for staying. Only Goshen was ahead of them, Goshen and its prized Hambletonian Stake to be raced a week from the following day.

Later, when Alec returned Bonfire to his stall, Henry said, "I'll tell you one thing about last night, Alec. With all those horses passin' Bonfire he should have learned that he's not goin' to be knocked down every time one goes by. It could have been the best thing that happened to him. It could have been better'n winning."

Alec said, "At least I got plenty of chances to open and close the eyecup. He's certainly used to that by now."

Henry studied Alec a long while. He wondered how much self-confidence Alec had regained from the previous night's race. "I guess we might as well pull out of here," he said a little later.

"You mean this afternoon?"

"I mean *now* . . . or just as long as it takes us to pack and load," Henry answered. "He's had a good walk and some grass. I'll take it slow with him."

"What about your car?"

"I'll come back for it later. No one will take it if I leave it here. Not unless they're pretty desperate."

"Okay," Alec said. And then he added lightly, "Goshen, here we come!"

A little over an hour later they were on their way in the light truck that was newly painted in Jimmy's red-and-white racing colors. The lettering on the sides read, "THE JIMMY CREECH STABLES, CORONET, PA." And below that, "BONFIRE, TWO-YEAR-OLD WORLD CHAMPION HARNESS COLT."

Alec sat beside Henry where he could watch Bonfire through the open window at the back of the cab. The colt was blanketed and had loaded easily. He was used to traveling from one county fair to another, and was taking this present trip with the ease and nonchalance of an experienced trouper. Alec watched him pull the hay from the sling in front of him and chew quietly while the truck picked up speed on the highway.

Alec glanced back at the high wire fence of Roosevelt

Raceway and the looming stands beyond. He knew that this would be his last look, for he wouldn't be coming here again—not as a competitor, anyway.

Soon the track was left behind, and Alec watched the mounting traffic as they approached the city limits of New York. In the distance, across from Long Island, he could see the towering skyline. They wouldn't have to go through the heart of the city. Henry had decided to cross the Bronx-Whitestone Bridge, avoiding much of the city's traffic. All the same, the trip wasn't going to be an easy one until they reached the rural country north of New York.

Henry grunted as he put on the brakes to avoid hitting a car in front of them. Alec glanced back at Bonfire. The colt was all right.

Finally Henry turned off the highway, taking little-used back roads that he knew from other years. Alec said, "Bonfire must have been quite an attraction at the county fairs."

Henry nodded. "I guess so. That's what Jimmy wanted. It's not often that folks on the small circuits get a chance to see a champion colt."

"That was nice of him," Alec said.

"Nice but not very smart," Henry answered. "Not when he expected so much from Bonfire in the Hambletonian."

Alec waited until a car had passed them before asking, "How 'short' do you think our colt is, Henry?"

"Plenty. He could use at least a month's more work before tacklin' a race like the Hambletonian." Henry paused, and then added, "If he was mine he wouldn't be goin' to the post. It's like tryin' to win the Kentucky Derby with a colt that can't go the full distance. This is worse, maybe, since he'll have to go at least *two* separate mile heats to win."

Alec looked straight ahead as they approached the bridge, noting the long span across the water to the Bronx and the boats beneath. But his thoughts were on Bonfire and Jimmy Creech. He knew how Tom had felt. Jimmy couldn't afford to wait for another colt, another Hambletonian. It had to be this year or not at all for him.

Traffic was light on the bridge and the truck rolled along smoothly. Alec looked at the colt again and then said, "You seem to know a lot about the Hambletonian."

Henry said, "It's my business to know any kind of racing."

"You said he'll have to go at least two separate mile heats."

Henry nodded. "It's not like the night raceways, where you go a mile dash and you're done. The Hambletonian is a gruelin' race against top colts. To win it a colt must win two heats out of three. If there are two different heat winners, they have to go a third mile. That's what makes it the classic it is . . . that and the hundred-thousand-dollar purse they're racin' for."

For a moment Alec was quiet. "He'll be able to go two fast miles, Henry. He went them last night before the race, you'll remember."

Henry glanced at him. "He'll need to go a lot faster than he did then and he won't be racin' alone. He can't make a slip and expect to beat those other colts."

"He won't make any slip," Alec said.

"I hope not. If he's goin' to win, he'll have to take those first two heats. I don't believe he'd be able to go a third mile, not at the speed at which it'll be raced."

"We'll make sure a third heat isn't necessary," Alec promised. They were at the highest point of the bridge, and beyond the teeming city Alec could see wooded hills. He wished that he felt the same confidence he had put into his words.

It was mid-afternoon when they neared the small village of Goshen, New York. Alec looked away from the rolling farmland and turned toward Bonfire. The colt had had an easy trip once they'd left the city behind. There'd been no traffic at all and Henry hadn't driven over thirty miles an hour at any time.

Alec looked out again at the fields of high corn and baled hay. It was a hot, sleepy afternoon but not a quiet one. The noise of tractors and mowers shattered the sun-drenched air. It was perfect hay-making weather with no sign of rain, and the farmers were taking advantage of it.

As his gaze traveled upward to the clear blue of the sky, Alec remembered his one other visit to Goshen. It had been Hambletonian Day of the only year his father had been able to get away from work and take him. Alec figured he must have been about nine years old. He remembered their sitting in the great stands, awaiting the Hambletonian. And then the black clouds had come, moving over the track and finally drenching it in a downpour. It had rained so hard the Hambletonian had been postponed until the following day.

After the announcement his father had opened the wicker picnic basket, offering him the chicken sandwiches Mom had packed. But he'd been too disappointed to eat, knowing his father's work made it impossible for them to return to Goshen the next day.

It had been his first truly great disappointment. He hadn't said a word all during the long drive home. He'd realized his silence was making his father, who'd tried so hard to please him, more miserable than ever. *How cruel can kids get?* Alec wondered now. Why hadn't he said, "It's all right, Dad. It was fun having the day off with you anyway." He'd been too young to have sense enough for that.

Alec glanced at the colt to make certain he wasn't in any trouble and then looked out at the passing scenery again. Well, he was returning to Goshen in a big kind of way, the like of which he'd never dreamed as a kid, even in his wildest dreams.

The truck turned off the highway, and Alec saw the huge outdoor poster with the picture of the old-timer leading a great, black horse. The man was small and bearded. He wore a floppy, wide-brimmed hat and a flowing black suit. Below the picture was printed: "HAMBLETONIAN STAKE—August 7—$100,000 Race."

They went down Goshen's narrow, tree-lined main street. Directly behind the old homes with their spacious lawns Alec could see the kite-shaped mile track of Good Time Park. No half-mile oval for Bonfire here but a track with three long straightaways. Alec was anxious to find out how his colt would take to this famed mile track. He was glad they were a week early for the big race.

Good Time Park was so much a part of this tiny village. There was no traffic on the street. Except for the children who watched them as they went by, Goshen was as quiet as that nearby stretch of track—and just as empty.

"Not much doing, is there?" he commented to Henry.

The old trainer grunted. "Plenty in the mornings," he answered. "Too hot to do anything now."

But at Roosevelt Raceway they'd be working, getting ready for the night's program, Alec remembered. The clock had turned around for them, and it seemed more right this way.

There were a few cars parked near the village square, where people sat drowsily on tree-shaded benches. For most of the year this was what Goshen was like. Only on Hambletonian Day would the village rock from the vibrations of many thousands of people descending upon it.

Henry turned the truck down a side street and approached the track gate. Stabled in the long sheds beyond were some of the world's most prized and valuable horses. Alec looked back at the village square. It seemed so right that in the sport of harness racing its most famous and richest classic should be held each year at Goshen. It was over this country-side that men had raced their horses long before the American Revolution, and only a few miles away was buried Hambletonian, the foundation sire of the harness-racing horse.

Henry stopped the truck just inside the track gate. "I'll find out where we're stabled," he said, opening the door.

Horses were being walked about the grounds, and some of them nickered. Bonfire answered, and his hoofs pounded the wooden floor beneath his straw bedding.

"Easy, Mister," Alec told him. "In a few minutes we'll have you out of there." He waited for Henry, wondering what was ahead of them in the days to come—*here* where everything would be decided for Bonfire and himself, for Jimmy and Tom and George and Henry. Five men and a colt—and a Hambletonian.

Classic Preview

11

The following morning Alec jogged Bonfire for the first time at Good Time Park. The sky was cloudy with rain forecast within a few hours. It seemed to Alec that almost all of the Hambletonian colts were working, their trainers taking advantage of the dry and fast track.

"But not Henry," Alec thought. "Bonfire and I are just out for a nice long jog." Henry had ordered five miles for them this morning, with no turning the right way of the track.

Alec didn't have much to do except to remember to close the eyecup whenever another jogging horse passed on Bonfire's right. But even that came instinctively now, so he spent most of his time humming to the colt and watching the other Hambletonian eligibles work their fast miles.

Lively Man was there with Fred Ringo driving him. So were Silver Knight and Victory Boy and Chief Express, all from Roosevelt Raceway. Their drivers were almost as young as Fred Ringo and looked just as tired. They had every right to be tired, Alec decided, knowing they'd flown from Roosevelt Raceway that morning to work their colts and would return to Roosevelt to race that night.

It was no life for an old man.

But there were old men here, lots of them, and some were driving top colts such as High Noon, Fibber and Bear Cat. They were men who had known and raced many a Hambletonian. Alec thought of Jimmy Creech and for a moment wished that Jimmy were sitting behind Bonfire. It was Jimmy's rightful place.

Bonfire seemed to like the wide, sweeping turns of the track and the three long straightaways. He was very alert this morning and most eager to be turned around when he saw the sweated working colts whip by. Alec kept telling him that he wasn't to be turned today. Maybe tomorrow. They'd have to wait for Henry to tell them. "He's running things, Bonfire."

But the blood bay colt didn't understand, especially when horse after horse passed, going the right way of the track.

Alec too watched them go, counting at least twenty Hambletonian colts on the track. If they all went in the big race next Wednesday there'd be a traffic jam all the way around. He hoped that he and Bonfire would be clear of it.

They passed the grandstand and bleachers that stretched the whole length of the home straightaway. Carpenters were mending broken chairs and boxes. "Railbirds" stood beneath the tall trees near the paddock gate, watching the horses. Alec saw these men turn and look at Bonfire because of the colt's red hood. They'd seen the eyecup close when a jogging horse had passed Bonfire directly opposite them a little while before.

"What you got on that colt?" one man called as Alec went by. Alec didn't answer. They'd find out soon enough. He saw Henry standing nearby, and the trainer yelled to him to move Bonfire a little faster.

Alec clucked to his colt and gave him more line. Bonfire took it readily and asked for more. He didn't get it and was furious with Alec all the way around.

Later back at the stables they washed Bonfire and Henry said, "He kind of lost his eagerness to go durin' that last mile, didn't he?"

"He didn't pull very much," Alec admitted. "I guess he was getting tired."

"He sure was. He's as sweated as they come. You'd think he'd been worked."

"Will you have me turn him tomorrow?" Alec asked.

"No. He's goin' to get a lot more joggin'. We'll go six miles at a faster clip than you went today. And there'll be more of that to come."

Alec kept working and said nothing. Later he walked the blanketed colt about the stable area. He paid no attention to such things as old and lovely trees whose leafy boughs brushed against him. Only Bonfire noticed the difference between this walk and the ones he had taken at Roosevelt Raceway, and he reached for the green leaves.

Alec knew he was being impatient in wanting to turn Bonfire the right way of the track. He realized Henry was right in making an attempt to build up their colt's stamina as much as possible in one short week. But Alec couldn't help wondering how Bonfire's speed compared with that of the other Hambletonian colts. He hadn't expected them to go so fast as they had this morning. If he worked Bonfire alongside them he'd know what to expect in the big race. But Henry wasn't going to let him turn Bonfire. He might as well forget it.

The next two mornings went a little easier for Alec in that the other Hambletonian colts were only jogged, so he didn't have to witness their extreme speed. So he too jogged his colt, watching the others and their drivers with eyes that sought out their good points and faults. And long after they'd left the track he continued jogging Bonfire the extra miles Henry had ordered.

He knew by this time that Lively Man, the roan son of Titan Hanover, was heavy-legged and wouldn't have to be feared greatly in the Hambletonian. What made him doubly certain of this was the fact that he was being driven by Fred Ringo. Ringo's high standing as a driver at Roosevelt Raceway had been earned because his stable consisted mostly of aged horses. He seldom rated his horses but pushed them from start to finish as fast as they'd go. Colts couldn't stand that kind of treatment, especially one like Lively Man. He'd collapse if Ringo tried it in the Hambletonian. And Alec was certain that Ringo wasn't going to change overnight, especially when the stakes were so high. He'd be out for the lead early and then attempt to stay there at any cost.

Silver Knight was more of a threat than Alec had thought at Roosevelt Raceway. The gray son of Volomite seemed to be taking very well to the mile track. It suited his long strides better than the half-mile oval.

But most of all Alec worried about the old men who sat so casually behind their Hambletonian colts. They were men whose faces showed no strain of the approaching race, and who joked freely with one another as they jogged along, mile after mile. Jimmy Creech would have felt at home with them. Indeed, he might have been one of them had it not been for his illness.

Saturday morning everything changed once more for Alec. It was work day for the Hambletonian colts, their last before the big race. Fred Ringo and the other raceway drivers arrived, having let their second trainers do the jogging for the two previous days. They all turned their colts the right way of the track. The old men no longer joked with one another.

Alec jogged Bonfire, and watched them go. He became more and more miserable as their speed increased and finally his gaze left them. *Why look at them?* he thought. *Why make it harder?*

When he had completed seven miles with Bonfire he went back to the barn. Henry noted his anxiety, and said, "Stop worrying about the others, Alec. Look at your colt. He's wet but you don't see much sweat on him. We're gettin' there all right. A few weeks more and we'd have it."

"But we have only three days," Alec said. "Aren't you going to let me turn him at all? He really wants to swing around and go."

Henry chuckled. "Let him wait for the Hambletonian," he said, ". . . and you too, Alec." He went around Bonfire and placed a hand on the boy's shoulders. "I don't mind you and him wantin' so much to turn. It's good, and when you do turn I'll be watchin' you, all right."

The big change came over Goshen Sunday night, for it was then that people began arriving for Hambletonian Week. The small hotel and inn filled rapidly, the overflow moving on to tourist homes and to hotels in nearby cities. But all this was only a mild tremor to the quake that would shake Goshen the following Wednesday. On Hambletonian Day would come thousands of people from all over the country, by special trains, planes and buses. Goshen would accept its heavy burden proudly and graciously, knowing that for a few hours it had come into its own again.

Monday morning the change swept quickly over Good Time Park. Great awnings of alternating orange and blue stripes extended over the bleachers and grandstand. Tents had been erected about the grounds and inside them prospered cake sales and church dinners. On the tall pole in the track's infield flew the blue-and-white flag of harness racing's "Grand Circuit."

Hambletonian Week had begun!

At noon Henry went to the race secretary's office and dropped a slip bearing Bonfire's name in the Hambletonian entry box. He also made out a check for the required five hundred dollars to start their colt in the race. And then he drew post position number 6.

When he returned to the barn Alec was anxiously awaiting him. "Well, we're in," Henry said. "Only about forty-eight hours to go now. Nothin' to it."

"What position did you draw?"

"A good one, *six*. We're in the first tier of ten colts with eight more starting behind us."

Alec said, "Then we've a good chance to get out in front of any jam."

Henry smiled. "I think so," he answered. "In fact, I think we got a better chance of doin' that than I have of collectin' from Jimmy the five hundred dollars I just had to put down for him."

Tuesday morning newspapers throughout the United

States carried the following story, filed directly from Good Time Park:

FIELD OF 18 TO RACE IN RICHEST HAMBLETONIAN TOMORROW

Lively Man Slim Favorite to Win $105,000 Race

Fastest Colts in History of Famed Hambletonian to Answer Post Call

---

BY "COUNT" CORNWELL

Goshen, N.Y., Aug. 6—The names of eighteen horses were dropped into the entry box for tomorrow's Hambletonian Stake, making this the richest of all prizes in harness racing's world famous classic with a gross value of more than $105,000.

There's talk going around Goshen today that not only will this Hambletonian be the richest in its long history but also the fastest. Never before have so many colts approached the classic race with such record-breaking times behind them. Nor have Goshen "railbirds" ever witnessed such speed as has been displayed by this year's Hambletonian eligibles in their clocked workouts during the past week in final preparation for the big one tomorrow.

For these reasons, together with the fact that few of the colts have met each other in competition this year, there is no odds-on favorite for the classic. Lively Man is liked by many who recall his spectacular victories at Roosevelt Raceway over Victory Boy, Chief Express and Silver Knight, all of whom will go to the post with him. The last-named colts have taken a liking to Good Time Park's kite-shaped mile track, as indicated by their record-breaking works. Silver Knight in particular has shown marked improvement over his half-mile racing form at Roosevelt. Perhaps this big gray colt needed the longer straightaways he has here. Or, perhaps, it was the switch in his drivers, for Paco DeBlois, second only to Freddy Ringo in the Roosevelt driver-standings, is now sitting behind him.

However, the old-timers who have spent day after day at the Goshen rail aren't impressed by the colts from the night raceways or the young, harried-looking men driving them. No, indeed. They'll tell you that Hambletonians are won by old boys like themselves, men who race their colts during daylight hours and usually on the "Roaring Grand," harness racing's Grand Circuit meetings at the big state fairs. They'll tell you that the colts to watch tomorrow are High Noon, Fibber, Bear Cat, Princess Guy,

Ghost Raider and Tangiers, all of whom are being driven by men over fifty years of age, men who have raced many a Hambletonian and know what to expect from their colts in order to win it.

Others here say to keep your eye on the colts who have been raced lightly this year and come mostly from the small-fair circuits. They'll tell you that these colts—Cricket, King Midas, Big Venture, Bonfire, Star Queen, Lord Bobbie, Mismatch, and The Saint—wouldn't be here at all if their trainers didn't have something cooking that might upset the heavily laden gold wagon of this year's Hambletonian. And the blazing time trials worked by these colts, with the exception of Bonfire, who's only been jogged, have added strength to their predictions.

So take your pick from this year's top three-year-olds—the night winners or day winners; the champions from the big state fairs or the small county circuits. They're all here at Goshen, and the hands taking them to the post tomorrow will be aged and experienced or young and deadly ambitious. The stakes are high—$105,000 and a place forever in harness-racing history.

The Party's Over

12

Tuesday evening the air was cool and pleasant but heavily laden with suspense, everybody waiting for Hambletonian Day to come.

"Let's get away from here for a while, Alec," Henry said. "We'll go to the inn and have dinner there. The change will do us good."

"But what about the colt?"

"I'll get someone to look after him," Henry returned. "There's an old guy just up the row who'll be glad to watch him for us. We won't be gone long."

Shortly afterward they walked out the police-guarded track gate. A few blocks away they saw a crowd assembled in the village square, where a small fair was going on. But Henry avoided it. "Let's eat first," he said.

"I'm not very hungry."

"We'll eat anyway," Henry answered.

They walked into the inn, which was just a block from the village square. The lobby and dining room were crowded

118

and noisy but they were soon given a table.

Henry sat down heavily, the light chair creaking beneath his weight. He looked around at the diners. "Just what we needed," he said. "A nice change." Turning to Alec, he saw that the boy was gazing intently at the horse pictures on the wall. "Stop looking at horses," he commanded. "We're supposed to be gettin' away from them. Look at the people . . . or your menu."

Alec picked up his menu, but all around him he could hear people talking about the coming day's race. He glanced at Henry. "We're not getting away from horses in this town tonight," he said.

"No, I guess not," Henry admitted. "But try not to listen."

After they'd given their orders to the waitress, Alec looked out the large window near them. Less than a hundred yards away was a half-mile track with a small grandstand beside it.

Henry said, "A town the size of a peanut and they have two tracks within a few blocks of each other. I don't think there's another place like it in the country."

"I guess that's why the Hambletonian is being raced here," Alec answered.

After dinner they found themselves walking toward the small track, and then alongside the rail to the stable area.

Henry grunted. "What'd we come this way for? We're supposed to be gettin' away from tracks and horses."

Alec laughed. "We found we couldn't. We gave up."

They walked up the road past the stables. Several Hambletonian colts were stabled here, and every morning they were led the few blocks to Good Time Park for their session on the big track.

An elderly man came out of the end barn. He could have been Jimmy Creech except that his face was unlined whereas Jimmy's was deeply wrinkled. "Howdy," he said, and when they stopped to talk to him he removed his peaked cap, running a hand around the stiff, white fringe of hair that ringed his bald dome. It made Alec think of George.

"Here's hopin' you have a good trip tomorrow," Henry said.

Not too good, Alec corrected mentally. For this man was Silas Bauder, winner of last year's Hambletonian, and tomorrow he'd be driving the top colt, Bear Cat.

"Same to you two," Silas Bauder replied, including Alec. "Y'got a nice lookin' colt, all right. But you ain't done much with him, have you?"

Henry said, "He'll do, I think."

"Sure he will," Bauder came back chattily. "There are a lot of good colts here, all right. Best year I can remember. It's goin' to be a real big party out there tomorrow." He laughed heartily.

"Where have you been racing, Mr. Bauder?" Alec asked.

"Don't go callin' me *Mister* Bauder. It's Si. I started Bear Cat early this spring in California with the rest of my stable, and then came here. Mile tracks only for him." He turned back to Henry. "Don't mind tellin' you that racin' mile tracks gives me a big advantage over most of you fellas an' your colts. You take a colt off the half-milers and put him on a mile track expectin' him to take to it right away. As a rule it doesn't work that way. It takes time, but no one seems to pay any attention to me when I tell 'em that."

"It makes sense to me," Henry said. "I'm listenin'."

Si Bauder smiled. "It's too late to do you any good tomorrow," he said.

"Yes," Henry agreed, "I'm afraid so."

Later they walked down the crowded streets of Goshen, and finally went up the steps leading to the long sweeping porch of the hotel. Henry led Alec to the far end, where it was comparatively quiet, and they sat down. They were still a part of all the noisy Hambletonian Eve activity but a little removed from it. For a long while they sat in silence, each concerned with thoughts that had nothing to do with all that went on in the street.

Alec's thoughts were of the fast quarter of a mile Henry had let him and Bonfire go that morning. Holding Bonfire down to the time Henry had ordered had been one of the most difficult jobs in his life. It had been so long since Bonfire had been turned that he'd wanted to go all out and all the way. As much as Alec had wanted to let him go, he knew that he had to hold the colt down, in order to conserve his speed and stamina for the big race the next day.

Henry removed his feet from the porch railing and said, "About that quarter-mile this morning."

"Yes?"

"After you'd gotten him slowed down an' that black mare passed you, weren't you a little slow in closing the cup?"

"Yes, I was," Alec admitted. "She surprised me . . . or I guess I was thinking too much about Bonfire's sprint. She was up beside me before I knew it. But it was all right. I closed the cup in time."

Henry said nothing. He put his feet back up on the rail, seemingly concerned with all that was going on in the street. But actually he saw nothing and he thought only of the problem that had been haunting him for a long while. So far as he was concerned, the right decision was more important than winning a Hambletonian. And he had less than twenty-four hours in which to make up his mind regarding that decision.

"Alec?"

"Yes, Henry?"

The old trainer didn't turn toward Alec. He looked only at his feet, bringing the tips of his shoes together and then apart again slowly. "I'd like your advice."

"You don't often ask for it," Alec said lightly.

"Sure I do." Henry paused before going on. "What happened to the colt when that black mare pulled up an' you didn't close the cup right away?"

"Nothing happened to him. I told you I closed it in time."

"But what if you hadn't?" Henry asked.

"You know what would have happened if I hadn't," Alec said in a surprised voice.

"No, I don't," Henry said abruptly. "That's why I'm askin' you. And I don't want you to go jumpin' to conclusions, either. Did you feel him tighten when that mare drew alongside and before you closed the cup?"

"No, he was steady," Alec answered quietly.

"An' tell me about all this past week while you were joggin' and bein' passed so often. Did you feel any fear or tenseness at all in him when they went by? You held the lines. You're the only one who'd know."

"No, I didn't feel anything like that," Alec said. "I'd forgotten about it, and so had he. The hood's responsible." He paused before going on. "I don't know what you're driving at, Henry. You know all this."

"I know what I see," the old trainer said, turning to Alec for the first time. "An' I think it's time we took off the hood." He looked at the boy a long while, waiting for him to speak.

Finally Alec said, "You don't mean tomorrow, Henry."

"Yes, I mean just that." When Alec turned away from Henry's close scrutiny the trainer went on, "From what I've seen and what you've told me I don't think he needs it any more. He's worn it in one race an' for many miles since then. He's got his self-confidence back. He knows he's not goin' to be knocked over whenever a horse passes him. So I say it's time to take it off."

"But why *tomorrow*, Henry?" Alec's voice was as low as it could be and still be heard.

"Tomorrow is as good a time as any," Henry answered. "Once a mechanical aid has done its job you take it off, an' the sooner you do it the better. If you don't, your horse gets so he really depends upon it an' ends up wearin' it the rest of his life." He stopped a few seconds and then added, "Look at it this way, Alec. It's a wise parent who takes a kid's glasses off when he doesn't need them any more. Leave them on an' his eyes get so used to them that he can never take them off. He's stuck with 'em for life. It's the same thing with the hood."

"But we can't take a chance *tomorrow*," Alec argued. "You've got to think of more than our colt. Think of Jimmy and George and Tom. They'll be here. We can't let them down."

There was no wavering in Henry's steady gaze. He could have said, "I'm thinking of them and *you* too." But he didn't. He didn't say a word because he didn't want Alec to know he was more concerned about him than he was about anyone else. He didn't like what he saw in Alec's eyes. He felt more confident about the colt than he did about Alec. Had Alec reached the point where he was depending upon the hood even more than Bonfire?

After a long while Henry turned away, saying, "Okay, Alec, if you feel that way about it. Forget what I said. I just wanted to talk to you about it."

A parade of boys and girls went by, chanting, "Here's to Goshen. . . . Go! Go! GO!"

Henry watched their snakelike parade weaving down the center of the street, while they waved signs and banners bearing the names of the Hambletonian colts. He'd already made up his mind what he was going to do.

He had wanted Alec's cooperation. He'd wanted him to agree to the removal of Bonfire's hood. But it hadn't worked out that way. Now he had to go it alone. He didn't know if it was fear *or* concern for the colt that was in Alec's eyes. It was important to find out. He wasn't going to take a frightened Alec back home with him. If it was fear, the place to lick it was here, and the time was *tomorrow*. After the Hambletonian it would be too late. Bonfire would be going home, and so would Alec.

Henry wouldn't let himself think of Jimmy Creech or Tom or George—or even Bonfire. Or the high stakes for which they'd be racing. His love and concern for Alec drove everything else from his mind. *"I'm playing for high stakes too,"* he mumbled to himself. *"Don't let me lose, please. Keep his hands light on those lines when he finds out that cord is of no use to him."*

"Did you say something, Henry?" Alec asked.

"No, nothin'. Just grumblin' to myself, I guess." Henry got to his feet. "Let's get back to Bonfire, Alec. The party's over."

Hambletonian Day

13

Bonfire was in the paddock by noon on Hambletonian Day. The other colts were there, too, all seventeen of them, as well as their drivers and owners and grooms. The day was cloudless and terribly humid but only Bonfire stood naked in his stall. The others wore cotton coolers, for they had just completed the first of their mile warm-ups in preparation for the race at three o'clock.

Henry looked around the crowded paddock. "Everybody's gettin' in the act today," he said with attempted lightness. "Owners an' their friends an' friends of friends."

Alec removed Bonfire's leg bandages and then rose and stood beside Henry. "I wonder where Jimmy went?" he asked.

"Probably to the box with Tom and George."

They had arrived early that morning aboard the special train from Pittsburgh. Tom had had no trouble getting around the stable area on his crutches, but George had insisted later that he go to their grandstand box rather than to the crowded paddock, where he might be knocked down and hurt. "It's enough that we got here at all," the old groom said. "Let's not push our luck too far."

Alec turned to Bonfire, who was pulling at his tie ropes and working up a lather. He knew he was going to race that day and he was getting impatient.

Henry said, "Put the cooler on him now, Alec."

In the next stall, number 7, was Bear Cat, and in front of him Si Bauder stood talking to a group of friends. A photographer took their picture.

Alec said, "I'd just as soon not have that colt where he is."

Henry nodded. "You'll really have to move Bonfire on the break to get out ahead of him." He turned and looked at the small black filly in the number 5 stall. "It won't be much better on the other side of you," he added. "Princess Guy won't be lagging behind, either. She's a fast little filly."

Shrugging his shoulders, Alec said, "At least we're in first tier with a *chance* of getting out in front."

"At least," Henry repeated, smiling. "We got nothin' to worry about, Alec. Relax."

"I'm relaxed. It's just this waiting that's hard to take." And Alec went into the stall to keep himself busy.

An hour passed and the Hambletonian colts left the paddock for their second warm-up. This time Bear Cat stayed behind with Bonfire. Henry glanced at the leggy brown colt standing in his stall, and then at Si Bauder, who was walking down the paddock row with his friends.

"I guess Si's skipping this one," he told Alec. "It's nice to have a little company."

"I'd rather have had him work Bear Cat," Alec answered.

"There you go worrying again," Henry teased.

Their side of the paddock was empty and quiet. But coming up the row were Jimmy and George and Tom.

"Like I said before, everybody's gettin' in the act," Henry muttered.

"Who has a better right than they?" Alec asked, a note of irritation creeping into his voice. He was touchy today but he supposed he had every reason to be. He didn't like all the responsibility he'd been given. To do his best with the colt was hard enough without having to think of what this race meant to the three now stopping in front of Bonfire's stall.

Jimmy said, "Tom wanted to take another look at him before the race and I figured it wouldn't be so crowded now."

Henry said, "Fine." He watched Tom, moving easily on his crutches, go toward Alec. Tom's eyes were saying everything that needed to be said. Earlier he and Alec had talked a great deal, but not now. It was no time for words.

Henry found that he couldn't take his eyes off them. Here was the youth upon which the sport of horse racing depended. He and the Jimmy Creeches and the Si Bauders were ready to be turned out to pasture, like aged racehorses. But they were leaving their sport in good hands—young and capable hands.

Tom had the determination and the courage to reach the greatest heights in harness racing. These were the essentials. It was true that he needed a little time—time to fill out his large-boned frame, time to rid himself of his impetuousness and the heavy sense of responsibility that had played havoc with his driving.

Standing beside Tom, Alec presented a striking contrast— a sleek greyhound compared to a gangling Great Dane. Oh, it was true that Alec's face disclosed all the responsibility that Tom's did. But the difference was that Alec wouldn't take it with him into the race. Once Bonfire stepped onto the track Alec would get down to the business of racing and think of nothing else. Instinctively he'd do everything right without thinking of anyone or anything but his colt. The many famous classics in which he had raced had made Alec a man long before his time.

Finally Henry turned away.

Beyond the paddock fence thousands upon thousands of people roamed Good Time Park while awaiting the first race on the Hambletonian Day Program. Some sat in the shade of towering trees, eating lunches from picnic baskets. Some ate in the big tents. And still others were already seated in the stands or standing at the track rail.

Over the public-address system the announcer said, "Ladies and gentlemen, may I have your attention? Warming up on track now are the Hambletonian colts. Passing the stands is Lively Man, being driven by Fred Ringo, who is Roosevelt Raceway's leading reinsman. This is Mr. Ringo's first Hambletonian.

"Behind and coming down close to the rail is Princess Guy, driven by Frank Lutz. Mr. Lutz is a veteran of twelve Hambletonians and the winner of one.

"Now turning and ready to come down the stretch are Silver Knight on the inside and Mismatch next to him, with Cricket and Tangiers trailing. I might explain to those of you who may be unfamiliar with harness racing that the purpose of these 'trips'—as we call them—is to limber up and steady the colts before they race. This will be a slow mile, perhaps no better than two minutes twelve seconds for most of the colts. The next mile, about an hour from now, will be faster.

"Silver Knight, passing the stands, is being driven by Paco DeBlois. Mismatch is being driven by . . ."

Jimmy had been listening to the announcer, but now he turned to Henry. "You think it's wise to send him out at all before the race?"

"No," Henry said. "We'll have Alec jog him going to the post . . . that's enough."

"How many heats do you figure he'll be able to go?"

"Two at the speed they'll be raced," Henry answered. "I'm hoping that's all we'll need to win. If we have to go a third heat it'll be rough on him."

"On all of us," Jimmy said.

They left just before the Hambletonian colts returned to the paddock. Alec pulled the cooler high on Bonfire's neck. He didn't especially care about watching the time-honored ritual about to take place, but there was nothing else for him to do. He turned to watch the colts, hoping it would make his waiting easier.

Harnesses were taken off their glistening bodies. Sponges washed away the sweat. Mild liniments were slapped on loose, sliding muscles. Manes and tails were brushed thoroughly. And then they were blanketed and put in their paddock stalls, to stand still and wait.

The races began, and while the time went faster for Alec his nervousness mounted. He knew it was no different for Henry or for any of the others in the paddock. It was impossible to be calm with the roar of the mobile starting gate in one's ears, the pounding hoofs, the race calls of the announcer, and always the shrill cries from the stands.

The Hambletonian colts completed their last warm-up directly after the first race. One hour to go now.

Henry glanced at Bear Cat often during that time, realizing Si Bauder had his colt ready to go the race of his life. Like Bonfire, Bear Cat was a light-boned, sensitive colt. And Si Bauder was one of the old leaders who long ago had understood the kind of colt he had and changed his training methods accordingly. Bear Cat hadn't gone out for that last warm-up, either.

Henry glanced at his watch and then went to Bonfire. He lifted the cooler, rubbing one hand over the wet coat.

Alec said, "He should go soon now. He's getting too worked up."

"Yeah, I know," Henry returned. There was a fine line between nervous energy and nervous exhaustion—in horses as well as in people. "When you get out there, jog him a slow mile," he told Alec. "But don't turn him, not until you're ready to go behind the gate."

Alec nodded, and a few minutes later the paddock judge called, "First heat of the Hambletonian. Get your colts ready!"

Alec whipped off Bonfire's cooler and the colt shook in his eagerness to go. He knew the time had come.

Henry slipped on the red hood, fingering the spring catch. It would be so easy to do now, so easy. All he had to do was to untie the cord from the catch. He looked at Alec.

A voice from behind said, "I couldn't just sit there in that box. Let me help." It was Jimmy, and he had the harness in his hands. He went into the stall with Alec.

Henry watched them. Jimmy was all thumbs with the harness. Alec did most of the work, trying to calm the colt at the same time.

"Get the bridle on him, Henry," Alec called anxiously. "What are you waiting for?"

Henry put on the colt's bridle while Alec and Jimmy lowered the shafts of the sulky in the rear of the stall. He saw Jimmy's deep-pitted eyes upon him. He saw all the hope and torment that was in them. And then he took the lines and the cord back to Alec.

I'll do it the next heat, he decided. *I'll let our colt get one winning heat behind him and then things won't be so tight around here.*

Alec drove Bonfire from the paddock with Jimmy walking beside him and Henry at the colt's head. He was glad they were moving, and thankful too for the shouting and bedlam on either side of the roped aisle to the track gate.

The marshal suddenly stopped the long line of Hambletonian colts. With the other drivers, Alec waited impatiently for the gate to be opened. Television cameras were trained on them, and the crowd pushed close, calling to the drivers.

A high voice shouted, "Who's going to win, Si? Who's it going to be this year? *You?*"

But the old veteran behind Alec did not answer or turn his head in the direction of the crowd. Instead he casually removed his false teeth and carefully wrapped them in a large handkerchief; then he placed them in the pocket of his green-and-yellow racing jacket.

"Better get those teeth back in before they take your picture in the winner's circle, Si!" a woman called. Everybody laughed except Silas Bauder.

Alec found that the laughter had helped. It eased the tension.

And then someone recognized Jimmy Creech. "What are you looking so nervous about, Jimmy? This is no different from the Butler Fair!"

Jimmy turned and faced the crowd. "I'm not nervous. I'm too old to be nervous." He tried to smile, and everybody laughed again.

This time the laughter didn't help Alec at all.

The track band was playing and Alec listened to the music. It might help more than anything else. The songs were associated with various states in the country and were being played in honor of the colts who represented those states. Alec heard the strains of the "Pennsylvania Polka." That was for Bonfire and Princess Guy.

Swiftly the tune changed to that of "California Here I Come." That was for Bear Cat and Mismatch.

Then the crowd was singing along with the next piece played, "Oh I come from Alabama with a banjo on my knee. . . ." That was for High Noon and Cricket.

"East Side, West Side, All Around the Town." That was for New York's Victory Boy and Chief Express and Lively Man.

"Back Home in Indiana." That was for Lord Bobbie.

"The Eyes of Texas Are Upon You!" That was for King Midas and The Saint.

"Carolina Moon." That was for Big Venture.

"Down by the Ohio." That was for Star Queen.

"My Old Kentucky Home." That was for Ghost Raider and Fibber and Tangiers.

And last of all the band played "Moon Over Miami" for Florida's gray colt, Silver Knight. Then the track gate opened and the announcer told a hushed audience, "Ladies and gentlemen, the colts are now coming onto the track for the first heat of the Hambletonian. This race is sponsored by the Hambletonian Society and today's purse is the largest in its long history, with a gross value of over one hundred and five thousand dollars."

Alec felt Jimmy's thin hand on his shoulder but the old man didn't say a word before leaving them. Henry stepped away from Bonfire as the colt went through the gate. "It's a cinch, Alec," he said easily.

Alec tried to smile back at Henry but found he couldn't. Nor could he say anything. His throat was too dry and tight. He drove Bonfire onto the track. They were alone.

The Hambletonian

14

Alec would have felt less alone on any other kind of track. His eyes left the harnessed colts for the two marshals who rode their palominos at the head of the post parade. They were his only touch with what he'd always known. For a second he wished that he were astride Bonfire rather than sitting behind him.

"Number one is Silver Knight," the announcer said, "a gray colt by Volomite out of Gray Dream. He is owned by Mr. Peter Conover of Venice, Florida, and is being driven by Paco DeBlois."

A favored colt starting from a favored position, thought Alec. *The luck of the draw was with him.*

"Number two," the announcer continued, "is King Midas, a chestnut colt by Hoot Mon out of Royal Maid. Owned by Mr. John Neville of Fort Worth, Texas, and being driven . . ."

Alec looked at the number 6 attached to Bonfire's bridle. He talked to his colt through the lines, telling him that they'd be jogging after the post introductions. It was a big field, as big as any in which Alec had ever raced. But this was different; there were eighteen sulkies behind the eighteen colts.

"Number five," the announcer was saying, "is Princess Guy, a black filly by Mr. Guy out of Little Mary. Owned by Miss Elsie Topper of Coronet, Pennsylvania, and being driven by Frank Lutz."

The large, heavy-set man in the sulky just ahead of Bonfire tipped his hat to the applause of the crowd.

And a different field, too, Alec thought, watching him, *in that many of these men are as old or older than Henry and still actively taking a part in the racing of their horses. Men who are young in heart and able to make good use of everything they've learned in the years behind them. It's not that way with jockeys. We take orders from such men, and try to fulfill them to the best of our ability. Just as I'm about to do.*

"Number six is Bonfire, a blood bay colt by the Black out of Volo Queen. He is owned by Mr. Jimmy Creech of Coronet, Pennsylvania, and is being driven by Alec Ramsay."

Alec touched his cap after the introduction, but his eyes didn't leave Bonfire. He knew he had three friends in those packed stands. It didn't matter if no one else knew him. This crowd was different, in a strange and inexplicable way, from the kind he had always known.

He clucked to Bonfire, letting him walk a little faster now that they had passed the judges' stand. "But I'm at home as long as I'm with you," he told this son of the Black.

Behind him he heard the announcer say, "Number seven is Bear Cat, a brown colt by Phonograph out of Meow. Owned by Mr. Allan Ullman of Los Angeles, California, and being driven by Silas Bauder."

The ovation that followed was unlike any of the previous

ones. It lasted all of a minute, and the announcer had to wait before going on with his introductions. Perhaps the long applause was for the tall brown son of Phonograph. But more likely it was for the little old man who was driving him.

Alec didn't turn back to look at Si Bauder. But if he had he was sure he'd have found an unsmiling face. Si wouldn't open his mouth, not with his false teeth wrapped safely in the pocket of his jacket.

The long line of Hambletonian colts continued to file past the stands, and only when they were far up the track did the marshals turn them loose. Then the announcer told the crowd, "The colts will take their usual two warm-up scores and then go behind the mobile starting gate for the first heat of the Hambletonian."

Unlike the others, Alec didn't turn Bonfire and take him past the stands at a fast clip. Instead he kept going up the track and around the far turn. He gave his colt enough line to jog at the speed Henry had ordered. Bonfire was moist without being sweated. His eagerness to be turned the right way of the track, *to go,* came across the long lines to Alec.

It was like holding two electric wires, and Alec delicately held the colt down without fighting him. He told him that soon they'd go, but first they must jog slowly to loosen up any muscles that might be a little tight.

They passed the cream-colored limousine with its great barrier wings folded at the sides. The starter was standing in the back waiting for the Hambletonian colts to complete their warm-up scores. He glanced in a puzzled fashion at Alec when Bonfire jogged by, but didn't say anything.

Up the long back straightaway to the second turn they

went and then around it, passing the half-mile pole and continuing up the backstretch toward the first turn. Alec looked beyond Bonfire at the colts who were stopping just off the turn and going back past the stands again. He let Bonfire jog a little faster, knowing the track marshals would be waiting to take them behind the gate at any moment.

"Here it comes!" he told Bonfire. "Here it comes!"

He should have felt more alone than ever going around the kite-shaped track with the great stands and horses in the distance, but he didn't. Somehow it had made things easier for him—and, he believed, for his colt. It had worked off that terribly nervous edge. Bonfire was ready to go, his muscles loosened by the slow jog. Whatever stamina he had was ready to be used in the long, grueling heats ahead.

Approaching the first turn, Alec heard himself humming to Bonfire for the first time. He knew then that he was as prepared as Bonfire to go behind the starting gate.

When they entered the homestretch, the other colts and the track marshals were waiting for them. Alec knew the marshals were angry at his holding them up but he didn't care. So far he had followed Henry's orders. He glanced at the long cord tied about his little finger. He'd almost forgotten it. He'd better remember it in the minutes to come. He'd be needing it, with seventeen other fast horses on the track.

The track marshals told him to hurry his colt into parade position. But Alec didn't hurry Bonfire. That would come later, behind the gate. The long line of colts went past the stands, and a marshal at either side of the track guided the colts in the first and second tiers. Alec drove Bonfire into his number 6 position. There were five colts in front of him and four behind him, making up the ten that would be starting in the first tier. Across the track were the eight colts in the second tier. At the head of the stretch the mobile gate awaited all of them.

Going past the grandstand boxes Alec heard someone shout his name. But he didn't take his eyes off the golden, empty track ahead; nor did the other drivers when their names were called out by the multitude. The time had come to race. It was written on the face of every driver, young and old.

After they had passed the mobile gate the barrier wings unfolded, stretching across the track. A short distance behind the gate the marshals let them go, and the announcer told the crowd, "The horses are now in the hands of the starter."

The colts in the first tier were the first to turn behind the gate, and Alec went with them. He'd known what to expect when Bonfire faced the right way of the track, and yet when the moment came it took all his skill to hold the colt. Only when Bonfire saw the barrier wings ahead did he slow his strides.

Standing in the back of the car, the starter called through the small microphone suspended from a leather strap about his neck, "Don't let your colt rush this gate, Ramsay! We're not going yet."

But the car *was* moving—slowly, it was true, but moving—and Bonfire pushed his red-hooded head close to the barrier in spite of everything Alec could do to keep him back. On either side of them the other colts in the first tier were coming up to the gate, while behind him Alec heard the rush of hoofs as the colts in the second tier followed closely.

The gate began moving faster and the starter's orders came faster as he tried to keep the large field in position. *No slips in this one. This is the Hambletonian. This must be done properly.*

Alec saw Bear Cat come up quickly on his right, the colt's brown head stretching for the barrier. Alec had no alternative but to close Bonfire's eyecup. Subconsciously he began to count off the seconds, knowing just how long he could keep the cup closed, and hoping desperately they'd be on their way soon so he could open it in time.

The car picked up greater speed going past the stands, but it wasn't going fast enough to suit Alec. Impatiently he looked ahead at the starting line while counting off the seconds. *Three ... four ...*

The thousands of spectators were on their feet. Eighteen colts moved as one, their hoofs drowning out the roar of the car's motor and the calls of the starter as he tried to hold them together for a short distance more.

Alec had experienced the thrill of surging power all around him in other races, but this was different. This was power controlled by one man and the moving barrier wings that held back the charging field.

"Fred Ringo!" the starter called suddenly. "Slow your colt down. You're almost on top of Ramsay!"

Alec didn't have to be told that Fred Ringo had his colt close to him. He could feel Lively Man's hot breath on his neck. The luck of the draw had given Lively Man the number 16 post position, a bad position for the Hambletonian favorite and his driver, who liked to get away in front. It was bad for Alec, too, because with Lively Man directly behind him he couldn't drop Bonfire back from Bear Cat and open the eyecup as he might otherwise have done.

Alec was worried. Eight seconds had passed and he still

had the eyecup closed, and now as they came within reach of the starting line another second went by. Then the barrier wings were swept away and the car whipped to the far side of the track. The roar of the crowd drowned out the starter's cry of "GO!" The Hambletonian was on!

Bonfire, free of the barrier wings and of Alec's restraining hands, bolted in a sudden surge of speed that swept him out in front. His red-hooded head appeared in front of all the others in that galaxy of straining bodies and brilliantly colored silks.

Alec asked his colt for more speed. He had to get away from Bear Cat on his right, and far enough out in front to feel safe in opening the eyecup. Ten seconds had passed. Never before had the cup been closed for more than twelve seconds.

Bonfire responded to Alec's urging. Alec saw Princess Guy's head drop on his left, but he didn't have room to cross in front of her to get away from Bear Cat. And the brown colt was staying with Bonfire, disclosing all the speed that Henry had said he possessed. Alec heard Si Bauder's shrill cries to Bear Cat and knew the old man wasn't going to let his colt drop behind.

Alec felt Bonfire's mounting uneasiness at the closed cup, and his own tension mounted until his heart was beating faster and harder than all those hoofs pounding toward the first turn. He tightened up on Bonfire, hoping to slow his colt in time to let Bear Cat go on ahead so he might open the cup. He could wait no longer; perhaps he had only a second more. He pulled back on the lines harder and then he was conscious of Lively Man's head directly above him. Ringo was following them, planning to go to the front with Bonfire!

The sweat poured from Alec's face and numbness swept over him. He couldn't take Bonfire back any farther with Lively Man on top of him! And it was too late to try once more to get ahead of Bear Cat. Already Bonfire was gathering himself, fighting the closed cup. Another stride and *he jumped high, twisting his body to the right*!

Fortunately Silas Bauder had seen Bonfire getting ready to jump. He pulled hard on Bear Cat, taking the three colts on his right out of the way with him while Bonfire came down and crossed in front of them; then Bauder and the other drivers turned their colts back, trying desperately to make up all the distance they'd lost. Ringo had taken good advantage of the near accident, having gone through the hole left by Bonfire's sudden jump and sharp swerve across the track. Now he had Lively Man where he wanted him to be, out in front of the crowded field!

Even with the eyecup open, Alec didn't get Bonfire under control until the colt came to a plunging stop in front of the outside rail. Bonfire was full of fury, and it would be many seconds before his anger would leave him. And yet Alec turned him back to the track. He had a race to run. He gave Bonfire more line, asking him for speed even though he knew it was hopeless to try and catch the others far down the backstretch.

He took him around the turn, and Bonfire's strides quickened at sight of the field far ahead of him. Alec's eyes became moist. Bonfire was fighting so hard to catch the others—and he didn't have a chance in the world.

He tried to tell his colt to wait, that there was another heat still to come when they'd have an even chance to win. But Alec wasn't allowed to pull too hard on the lines or sit too far back in the sulky. The judges wouldn't let him rest his colt. Bonfire must go a fast mile along with the others. There could be no jogging, no conserving of stamina and speed for the next heat. That was the rule of the race, and Alec could only plead with his colt, fingering the lines lightly, asking him not to try so hard.

Bonfire didn't understand. He pushed his hooded head forward, demanding more rein than he was being given. He went long and low and swift, ever closing the distance between him and the colts trailing the large field. But even these were well down the back straightaway when Bonfire rounded the second turn, passing the half-mile pole. His strides came faster as he tried to close the gap still more.

Alec gripped the lines hard, fighting his colt, holding him down as much as possible. But Bonfire had waited to be turned the right way of the track for too long a time, and there was no stopping him now. Yet Alec never gave up trying, even when they swept into the homestretch with the last of the field still many lengths in front.

Bonfire caught one lone straggling colt before he went under the finish wire. And that was *his* victory.

Over the public-address system the announcer said, "The unofficial order of finish for the first heat of the Hambletonian is as follows: The winner, Lively Man; second, Princess Guy; third, Silver Knight; fourth, Mismatch; fifth, King Midas; sixth, Cricket; seventh, Bear Cat; eighth, High Noon; ninth, Tangiers; tenth, Star Queen; eleventh, Fibber; twelfth, Lord Bobbie; thirteenth, Ghost Raider; fourteenth, Victory Boy; fifteenth, Chief Express; sixteenth, Big Venture; seventeenth, Bonfire; and eighteenth, The Saint."

At the first turn Alec stopped Bonfire along with all the other colts. He turned and went back up the track to hear the announcer say, "Ladies and gentlemen, the results are now official. Mr. Ringo, please bring your colt before the judges' stand."

As Alec drove Bonfire toward the track gate, the announcer said, "Ladies and gentlemen, introducing the winner of the first heat of the Hambletonian: Lively Man, a roan son of Titan Hanover and Blue Maid . . . and his driver, Fred Ringo."

The applause was loud and long but Alec didn't listen. He drove Bonfire to where Henry awaited them.

Backfire!

15

Henry led Bonfire back to the paddock. There were few people in their way, for most of them were still at the track watching Lively Man and Fred Ringo.

"It was a tough break, Alec," and that was all Henry said about the race.

Bonfire was stripped of his harness. Henry washed him. He cleaned his wide dilated nostrils, helping him to get all the air he needed after his hard, discouraging mile. He slapped on the mild liniment and then covered him.

Meanwhile Alec sat in a chair watching Henry and breathing as heavily as the colt. He turned to Si Bauder, sitting in front of the next stall. The old man's face was white and his mouth sagged. Si hadn't put back his teeth yet. His eyes were on the number 16 stall across the row. Lively Man was being washed by grooms, and standing around him were newsmen and photographers.

As Alec turned back to Henry his friend said, "I wish

you'd opened the cup. Like I told you last night, I don't think he needs it closed any more."

Alec said nothing.

Henry pulled the cooler high up on Bonfire's neck. "If you had, it couldn't have been any worse than it was."

Alec made no comment for a while and then he said, "It could have been a lot worse."

Henry got the lead shank and walked Bonfire. "Take it easy, Alec," he said going past the boy. "I'll just move up and down the row awhile."

Alec nodded. He watched Henry lead Bonfire through the crowded area. He heard the old trainer's repeated warnings to those in his way. "Horse coming! Horse coming!"

Most of the other Hambletonian colts had been blanketed and were now standing cross-tied in their stalls. Alec saw the paddock judge stop Henry and for a few minutes there were heated words; then Henry continued up the row.

When he came back, he told Alec, "That guy tried to tell me I couldn't walk my horse. I told him we weren't goin' to do any racing if we couldn't walk. I guess he'll leave us alone . . . 'as a special favor to a Hambletonian colt,'" he added bitterly. "That's what he said."

After Henry had gone Alec thought of Jimmy and Tom and George. It looked as if they weren't coming to the paddock between heats. Perhaps they'd decided it would be too crowded a place for Tom. More likely it was because they didn't want to face him or Henry. Especially Jimmy. Jimmy had no reason for not being here except his great disappointment. Alec bit his lip. Perhaps it was just as well. It would be hard for him to look at Jimmy.

Henry came down the row again, but this time he stopped

before the next stall as Si Bauder said, "You're a walkin' fool, Mr. Dailey."

Henry grinned. "It's easier than sittin' and better for the colt, Mr. Bauder."

"You'd never get away with it if we all got out there and started walking our colts."

"No, I guess not," Henry said, looking around him. "Paddocks should be built with horses in mind, not people."

"You got funny ideas, Mr. Dailey."

"An' some of yours are funny to me, Mr. Bauder." Henry glanced at Bear Cat. "Your colt's blowin'. He'd get more air out from under that low roof." He began walking away, and then stopped to look back. "Tell me, Mr. Bauder, why do you walk a horse after a race and yet let him stand hot in his stall after a heat?"

"I'll think that one over, Mr. Dailey."

Henry continued walking Bonfire, and the long minutes passed. From the track came the roar of the starting gate and the pound of horses as another race began.

During the next half-hour Henry passed Silas Bauder often but nothing more was said. Alec got up from his chair and began walking beside Henry and the colt. His tension was mounting now that the time for the second heat was approaching.

"I'll walk him, Henry."

"No, take it easy, Alec. You've got enough to do."

"I guess Jimmy's not coming back."

"I guess not."

"Henry—"

"Yes, Alec?"

"We'll be starting from a bad position this next heat."

"Not so bad," Henry returned lightly, trying to relieve Alec's tension. "You could have finished last and been starting from the eighteenth position."

Alec smiled. "It might have been better, then I could've gone around on the outside."

"You can still race on the outside if you want to, Alec." Henry turned to the boy, watching him closely. "Or you can drop back and go over to the rail, then look for holes comin' up on the inside. It's the shorter way." Henry didn't add *"but the most dangerous."* He didn't have to, for Alec knew.

They walked on in silence with only the sound of Bonfire's light hoofs ringing in their ears. Finally Henry brought the colt to a stop and felt beneath the cooler. "Let's put him in the stall now," he said.

Later, while they worked around Bonfire, Henry glanced at the red hood hanging at the side of the stall. No matter what route Alec decided to take in the next heat, the hood wasn't going to be of any use to him. Henry realized he'd be taking a long chance in disengaging the cord from the spring catch but he had no alternative. He must have faith in his belief that neither Bonfire nor Alec needed this mechanical aid any longer. And it had to be this heat. If Lively Man won again, there wouldn't be another.

Alec said, "I don't think Lively Man will last this next heat. Ringo will go all out again. The colt will fold on him in the stretch."

"Maybe an' maybe not," Henry returned. "He'll be going away from the pole position. He should have an easier time of it than before."

"Then you think he'll win?"

Henry shrugged his shoulders. "I don't know. They're all

top colts, Alec. I'm talkin' about starting positions. What happens after they get away is something else again." He brushed Bonfire's long forelock. "It's not just Lively Man and Ringo we have to worry about."

"But if he wins, it's over."

"I know it, and if we win we'll still have to go a third heat."

Alec rubbed Bonfire's nose. "Do you think he'll be able to go a third heat?"

Henry smiled grimly. "Go out and win the second first. Then we'll start talkin' about the third."

No more was said until the call came for them to get the colts ready for the second heat of the Hambletonian. Henry helped Alec with the harness and said, "My advice is to follow Bear Cat, who'll be startin' right in front of you in the Number Seven spot. I got an idea that Bauder will be findin' holes for his colt this time, and you can go through with him. Si isn't very happy about young Fred Ringo bein' in the limelight. He'll be out to put 'im in his place. You go along with Bauder, and then turn Bonfire loose comin' for home. We'll see what happens then."

"Okay, Henry," Alec said.

Henry stepped to the front of the stall to get the red hood. He saw Si Bauder impatiently snapping his long whip at small pebbles on the ground while Bear Cat was being harnessed. Henry heaved a sign of relief at the thought that all he had to do was to give advice in this race. He was too old for anything else. So were Bauder and a lot of the other men about to get in their sulkies. But they wouldn't admit it.

Henry removed the red hood from its peg, and held it in his hands for a moment. He touched the leather eyecup and the spring catch to which the cord was attached.

"Hurry up, Henry," Alec called from within the stall. "The others are going out."

"Comin'," the old trainer said.

He slipped the hood on Bonfire's head and the bridle over it. He fastened the lines to the bit and then, removing the cord from the spring catch, tied it to the bridle where it would do Alec and Bonfire no good whatsoever. Then he took the lines and cord back to Alec.

They had Bonfire hitched to his sulky and out of the stall when Jimmy Creech came hurrying up to them.

"I couldn't get away until now," he said awkwardly. "I thought it'd be better if I stayed with Tom."

"Sure," Henry said. "We figured that."

The line started moving and Bonfire, wearing his number 6, followed Princess Guy. Behind him came Bear Cat with Silas Bauder walking beside the sulky.

Jimmy dropped back to Alec's side. "We got a tough break that first heat. But it'll be different for us this time."

Jimmy didn't look at Alec while he spoke, but the boy was aware of his disappointment. Jimmy was trying hard not to disclose his true feelings. He talked all the way down the paddock and through the roped aisle to the track gate. Alec listened to him but said nothing. What he and Bonfire did on the track was all that mattered now. Only actions, not words, could change things from the way they were.

The colts were brought to a stop at the track gate, and there they awaited the bugle call to the post. Jimmy left Alec to go to Henry, who was at Bonfire's head. He talked to him a moment, his small, sad eyes searching Henry's for some sign of encouragement.

Henry couldn't give Jimmy the assurance he wanted, for he wasn't certain of anything himself. "We got a fast colt," he finally told Jimmy because his old friend expected him to say something. "He's as fast as anything goin' out there, maybe faster . . . but we don't know. A lot depends on the kind of breaks we get this time."

"You're right, Henry," Jimmy said. "I know I've got a Hambletonian colt. As you say, what happens depends on the breaks we get. I got to look at it that way."

His eyes remained on Bonfire until the post call came over the public-address system. The track gate was opened and the marshals astride their palominos took charge of the colts.

Jimmy began stroking Bonfire's sleek neck. Suddenly he stopped. "Look, Henry," he cried, "the cord's not fastened to the catch!" He held Bonfire back while the five colts ahead of him went through the gate. The marshals waited impatiently for Bonfire to follow.

Sitting in the sulky seat, Alec watched Henry while Jimmy tied the cord to the spring catch. Finally Henry turned to him and their gazes met. Each knew the other was aware that the oversight had been intentional. Alec's eyes glittered with anger, while Henry's were clouded with disappointment.

"Ladies and gentlemen," the announcer said, "the horses are now coming onto the track for the second heat of the Hambletonian."

Alec drove Bonfire through the gate without a word to Henry.

Red Heat

16

Alec found that his anger was only making Bonfire uneasy during the post parade. He tried to forget Henry and his foolhardy act at this stage of the Hambletonian. He steadied his hands and concentrated on the race to come. They must win. This was their last chance.

"Ladies and gentlemen," the announcer said as the colts filed past the grandstand, "the starting positions for the second heat of the Hambletonian will be those which the horses earned in the first heat." He paused, waiting for the track marshals to pass the judges' stand. "Number one is Silver Knight, driven by Paco DeBlois, who finished third in the previous heat and will therefore be starting from the third post position in this heat.

"Number two is King Midas, driven by John Neville, who finished fifth in the first heat and will now start from the fifth position.

"Number three . . ."

Alec glanced at the great stands. Somewhere in the boxes

near the front were Tom and Jimmy and George. They were no doubt wondering, as he was, if he could get Bonfire clear of the big field from his bad starting position.

The announcer was saying, "Number five is Princess Guy, driven by Frank Lutz, who finished second in the first heat and will start from the second post position.

"Number six is Bonfire, driven by Alec Ramsay, who finished seventeenth and will start from that position in the second heat."

Away back in the second tier. Not good. Not good at all. Would they get a chance even to race? "Follow Bear Cat," Henry had said. "—Bauder will be finding holes for his colt this time, and you can go through with him." Could he?

"Number seven is Bear Cat, driven by Silas Bauder, who finished seventh in the first heat and will start from that position."

The announcer didn't give the crowd a chance to applaud very long for Bauder, and went on with the introductions. Only when he'd reached the sixteenth colt in the post parade did the loud clapping from the stands prevent him from continuing after he'd said, ". . . Lively Man, driven by Fred Ringo, winner of the first heat and starting from the pole position."

Ringo touched his cap and smiled in acknowledgment of the long outburst from the crowd. Yet his face held none of the enthusiasm he had shown in the paddock. He knew he had to take this heat too in order to win the Hambletonian.

The track marshals turned the colts and their drivers loose at the top of the homestretch. Alec continued around the far turn, going the short quarter-mile jog that Henry had ordered. He waited until the others had completed their second warm-up score past the stands and then turned his red colt around. Bonfire's ears pricked forward and his strides quickened when he faced the right way of the track. But he didn't fight Alec going slowly down the homestretch. He knew what was to come. He awaited the barrier wings. He knew they would soon be in front of him. Alec didn't have to tell him.

The Hambletonian colts came back up the stretch in two separate columns, just as they had done before the previous heat. But this time they took their earned starting positions. Alec took Bonfire behind the sixteenth horse, Big Venture. Across the track from him were the colts starting in the first tier. Lively Man led the way.

They filed on both sides of the mobile starting gate and then turned behind it. It moved away from them and the colts in the first tier went faster.

Alec started Bonfire slowly, making no attempt to pull up behind Bear Cat in a hurry. The other colts in the second tier were already in position.

"Bring up your colt, Ramsay!" the starter called.

Alec moved Bonfire a little faster going past the bleachers. The colt wanted more line and his demands became more insistent. Alec didn't give in to him. He didn't want to have to close the cup at the start again. He kept him just behind the second tier of colts, in a position left open between Big Venture and The Saint.

The starter didn't call out to Alec again. He was having enough trouble with the colts and drivers in the first tier.

"Ringo, you're rushing the gate. Keep your colt back or I won't send you off!"

Across the tightly packed field of horses Alec could see

Lively Man's nose touching the barrier. Ringo kept him there, determined not to lose the favored rail position. He was leaning far forward in his seat in a strained attitude, the picture of determination and ambitious youth. He paid no attention to the starter's orders, taking a chance that this race was much too big and important for a recall.

The car's speed increased and with it the beat of hoofs. Alec saw The Saint on the far outside begin to fall behind the second tier; his driver was already having trouble with him. Alec gave Bonfire more line, going ahead of The Saint now that he'd have racing room on his right and wouldn't have to close the cup. Bonfire pushed his head close to Silas Bauder's back and Alec kept him there. *Break number one had come with The Saint's refusal to stay up with the others in the second tier.*

They pounded past the grandstand with the starting line only a short distance away. Faster went the gate and the colts behind it. Alec kept his eyes on Bauder's green-and-yellow jacket. The little old man sat easily behind Bear Cat, his shoulders hunched forward but showing no tightening, no strain. Alec wished his own shoulders were as free. Bauder didn't seem as anxious to get away in front as Henry had said he'd be. Bear Cat had his head behind the other colts in the first tier. Alec glanced at High Noon, Tangiers and Star Queen on Bear Cat's right. He hoped one of them would lag behind at the break so he could get Bonfire alongside Bear Cat, then go around the field.

But it looked as though there'd be no going around. Henry had said, "Follow Bear Cat," and that's what he'd do. He'd come a long way listening to Henry's advice. He wasn't going to stop now. *But come on, Bauder. Get your colt closer to the gate!*

There was no change in Bear Cat's position until the last few strides before the start. Then Bauder's thin shoulders moved forward slightly and his hands came up. Bear Cat's strides lengthened gradually, his speed mounting. He was still behind the other colts in the first tier, all of whom had their noses close to the barrier. But Bear Cat was coming up to the gate in a rush, and Alec knew then that the little old man sitting behind him was timing his colt's strides to co-incide with the opening of the gate.

Bauder's strategy was perfect! When the barrier wings swept away he had Bear Cat going at top speed. The brown colt went across the line faster than any of the others in the first tier. But behind him Bonfire came as fast, his red-hooded head close to Bauder's green-and-yellow silks.

The second heat, perhaps the final heat of the Hambleto-nian, had begun!

The cries of the drivers rose above the beat of hoofs. Alec remained silent, his eyes on Bonfire and Bauder's silks. He knew Bear Cat was well out in front, for to his own left and right were the colts in the first tier. He glanced at High Noon, racing so near on his right, and closed the eyecup.

Bauder's calls to his colt came back to Alec. Just as Henry had said, the old man was "out to put Ringo in his place." For a few seconds Bauder was beating Ringo at his own game. He was out in front and determined to take the pole position away from the young raceway driver.

Alec shoved his feet hard against the iron stirrups on the shafts. He gave his colt more line, ready to go on with Bear Cat to the front. Bauder's early drive was everything he and Henry could hope for. If it lasted, it would get Bonfire away from the packed field with a chance to race his best. That was all Alec asked.

Ringo was driving Lively Man hard. The roan colt was in front of the others but half a length behind Bear Cat. Alec saw Ringo go for his whip. The raceway driver was determined not to let Bauder take the rail position from him. It was a driver's duel between Ringo and Bauder! The crowd was aware of it, and Alec heard the pandemonium that burst from the stands as the sulkies whipped by.

Bear Cat's speed mounted on the way to the first turn and Alec kept Bonfire directly behind him. High Noon had dropped back and the eyecup was open again. With the exception of Lively Man, Bonfire was out in front of all the colts in the first tier! Bauder was far enough ahead to start crossing over to the rail as they rushed into the first turn. Alec followed him.

Together they closed in on Ringo with Bear Cat a length ahead. Alec saw Ringo go for his whip again, trying to keep Bauder from slipping Bear Cat in front of him. But Bauder wasn't to be denied. He asked for more speed from his brown colt, and Alec urged him on!

Bauder was not being a patient old man, rating his colt and waiting for the breaks to come his way. As ambitious and determined as Ringo, he was making his own breaks.

Alec wanted no driver's duel with Ringo for himself. That could come later, if necessary. He was getting what he wanted. Bonfire was clear of the packed field and the open track was before him.

Going into the turn, Bear Cat took the rail from Lively Man. But Alec made no attempt to draw alongside Bear Cat and pass him. Instead he stayed just off the rail with Bonfire, and to his left raced Lively Man, now in a tight pocket!

Alec didn't have to look at Ringo to sense the fury that

must be in the raceway driver's face with Bear Cat directly in front of him and Bonfire on his right.

Sulky wheels screamed taking the strain of the turn, while behind Alec came the ever pounding hoofs of the large field and the distant roar of the crowd. Alec listened to nothing but the low, steady beat of his own colt's hoofs. Ahead of Bonfire was empty track with all the racing room he needed. He could not have asked for more! It wasn't necessary to tell this to his colt, for Bonfire's head was stretched forward eagerly, his ears pricked.

Bauder slowed Bear Cat, resting him now that the early sprint was over and he had the rail. He glanced back to see who was just off to his right. When he saw Bonfire's head he turned away.

Alec slowed Bonfire too, content now to play Bauder's patient game of resting and rating his colt. He glanced at Ringo. The young driver was furious at being forced to slow his colt, to stay behind with no way out of the pocket. Behind them came the thundering field and for Ringo there was no dropping back and coming around Alec and Bonfire. He had lost his chance.

Over the public-address system came an announcement which Alec heard. "At the quarter-mile," it said, "it's Bear Cat out in front with Lively Man and Bonfire racing head and head. Then it's Silver Knight, Princess Guy, Tangiers, Cricket, Mismatch, King Midas, Fibber . . ."

Alec listened, aware of what it must be like back there in the packed field.

They started down the backstretch, and the pounding hoofs of the field came ever louder and closer. But Alec didn't move Bonfire any faster. He was content to stay where he was for the time being, confident that Bauder was the man to beat. The old man was being very canny. He was regulating the pace to suit his brown colt. But he knew also what he was doing to Fred Ringo.

Alec heard a horse coming up on his right, and then he saw Princess Guy's small black head. Bonfire heard her too and demanded more rein. But Alec waited, refusing to give in just then. He told his colt it wasn't yet time. Princess Guy drew alongside and Alec closed the eyecup. He let the filly move ahead, watching portly Frank Lutz make his bid for the lead. Then he opened the eyecup again and gave Bonfire the line he wanted. They moved up a little, keeping Princess Guy on the outside with not enough room to cross in front of them.

Silas Bauder watched the filly too, as anxious as Alec to keep her on the far outside. He moved Bear Cat faster going down the backstretch, maintaining his lead.

Alec was content with his position. There was still open track before him. He had room to take Bonfire between Bear Cat and Princess Guy, if he wanted. But he held Bonfire back, content with the pace set by Bear Cat which was just right for Bonfire.

At the middle of the backstretch he saw Ringo glance behind and then slow his colt, dropping from Alec's sight. Alec knew Ringo was taking Lively Man out of the pocket and would come around on the outside. It was what he had expected. It would probably work but at the expense of extra effort and stamina from Lively Man.

Suddenly Silver Knight came up on the outside with a tremendous burst of speed that swept him past Princess Guy and Bonfire. Concern came to Alec's eyes when he saw Silver

Knight move out in front, with Bauder letting him take the rail from Bear Cat!

Race strategy was now becoming more complicated and called for quick decisions. Bauder moved Bear Cat off the rail and directly in front of Bonfire. Alec looked at those green-and-yellow silks in front of him. No longer did he and his colt have an open track. Bonfire began fighting him, and Alec knew his colt was as anxious as he was to go on. He tried telling himself and his colt to be patient, that there was plenty of time. But it was becoming more and more difficult for him to stay behind.

Setting the pace was Silver Knight. Just to his right was Bear Cat, racing neck and neck with Princess Guy, who had moved up. Bonfire followed Bear Cat. The rail position directly behind Silver Knight was open, but Alec wanted no part of it. He preferred to be where he was with a chance to follow Bear Cat or go around Princess Guy, if necessary. He kept glancing back to his right. He didn't want any colt to come up and box him in behind the colts in front.

But it was on his left that the next move came. Mismatch pounded through on the rail, passing Bonfire and going up behind Silver Knight. Now Mismatch, Bear Cat and Princess Guy were racing stride for stride.

"Come on, Bauder," Alec mumbled to himself, anxious and more concerned than ever now, "make your move." If Bear Cat went on, Alec could follow with Bonfire and leave the other colts behind. But Bauder wasn't ready to make his move. The old man seemed to be content to stay where he was.

They swept into the second turn, and it was then that Alec knew he couldn't remain behind Bear Cat any longer.

Far on the outside came Lively Man and Fred Ringo! Racing wide around the turn, Ringo passed the others and took the lead from Silver Knight!

The announcer's call came through the loudspeakers in the track's infield, reaching the drivers. "At the half-mile it's now Lively Man in front with Silver Knight second, then Mismatch, Bear Cat and Princess Guy racing together. Bonfire is next, *and moving up fast is King Midas!*"

Alec heard no more, for King Midas was alongside him. He closed the cup quickly. No longer did he have a chance to pull out and around Princess Guy as he'd intended to do when they came off the turn! King Midas stayed behind the black filly, his driver wanting to go no wider than necessary around the turn.

Pocketed with the eyecup closed.

Fearful now, Alec listened to his heart pound out the seconds while he tried to decide what to do. He knew it would depend on what happened all around him. They were coming off the second turn with the long back straightaway before them. Certainly it would be here that Bauder would make his bid with Bear Cat. The old man couldn't wait any longer, with Lively Man and Silver Knight racing ahead of him!

But Bauder kept his brown colt even with Mismatch and Princess Guy, making no attempt to catch the leaders two lengths ahead.

Alec felt the first signs of uneasiness sweep over Bonfire. The cup had to be opened soon! He glanced at King Midas and found the colt was being taken outside and around Princess Guy. Relieved, Alec opened the cup, determined to follow King Midas. No longer would he keep Bonfire behind all these fast colts, waiting for Bauder to make his move.

It was then that Bear Cat was given more line! Alec shifted direction quickly and went behind him again. Bonfire took all the rein Alec gave him and asked for more. He followed Bear Cat as the brown colt caught and passed Silver Knight. But Princess Guy stayed with them a head behind Bear Cat, a stride in front of Bonfire. Alec stayed behind Bauder, knowing that soon the filly would be giving way before this extreme speed. Her strides were shortening even now.

A length in front of Bear Cat and on the rail raced Lively Man, with Ringo getting all the speed he could from his lathery colt. It wasn't enough, for Bear Cat was moving up on him fast. Alec knew how much speed Bauder's colt had left. And he knew too that Bonfire was equal to any kind of a race with him. The rated pace and Henry's training methods were about to pay off! Princess Guy dropped back a little more as they all swept past the three-quarter-mile pole and went into the final turn. The black filly was holding up under a last hard drive by Frank Lutz, but it wasn't going to be enough.

The last call rang through the loudspeakers. "With a quarter of a mile to go it's Lively Man still in front and under a hard drive. Bear Cat is second, followed by Princess Guy and then Bonfire. Mismatch and King Midas are going wide around the turn. High Noon, Fibber and Lord Bobbie are making their bid on the rail. Victory Boy and . . ."

But Alec wasn't listening. All that mattered were the two colts and filly in front of Bonfire. They came off the turn and there it was, the final stretch of track!

He glanced nervously at Princess Guy again. She was

holding on better than he'd expected. It was too late to go around her now. Bear Cat was beside Lively Man. Ringo was using his whip, trying to keep his tired colt up in front. Stride for stride Lively Man and Bear Cat raced. They started past the bleachers.

Sweat poured from Alec's face and ran into his eyes and mouth. It was now or never for Bonfire—for himself, Henry, Jimmy, Tom and George. They were there somewhere, in that distant blur of faces, watching, waiting, hoping. *If that black filly just wouldn't hold on so hard. If she'd only drop back a little faster and give him racing room to go between her and Bear Cat.* Bonfire had the speed to go on. But there was no place for him to go. If they lost, Alec knew the fault would be his alone.

They approached the first seats of the grandstand. Bauder was having his troubles too, for Lively Man was holding on as Alec never had thought he'd be able to do. The roan colt stayed with Bear Cat under Ringo's forcing, unrelenting drive for the wire. The eyes of thousands were on them, knowing what these last few yards meant to each of them. For Ringo, the Hambletonian in his very first attempt! For Bauder, another chance to win the Hambletonian in the third heat!

Inch by inch Bear Cat went ahead of Lively Man to the tremendous roar of the crowd. Behind the two leaders Princess Guy faltered and shortened stride still more.

Alec closed the eyecup as the filly raced head and head with Bonfire. Bear Cat now was a half-length in front of Lively Man in a final drive to victory! Alec went ahead with him, keeping Bonfire's nose above Bauder's green-and-yellow cap. And then Princess Guy no longer raced on their right.

Alec gave Bonfire the long-awaited command, taking him around the silks that had been constantly before him. The blood bay colt responded quickly, eagerly, and now there was nothing before him but empty track!

They'd gotten out in time. Alec gave Bonfire full line, urging him on with heart, hands and voice. Now it was up to his colt!

The stands were aware of this new challenge to Bear Cat seconds before it dawned on Silas Bauder. The old man saw Bonfire only when the blood bay colt was *alongside*! He urged Bear Cat to meet this sudden dangerous threat. Bear Cat responded to his demands but not before Bonfire had reached the very peak of his speed. As one horse they took those last great strides, their heads stretched forward, their glistening, sweated bodies strained to the utmost. Seemingly they swept beneath the finish wire together!

Alec decreased Bonfire's speed slowly, and went far beyond where Silas Bauder stopped Bear Cat. He wanted to be alone with his colt. He felt terribly weak, and was hardly able to sit in his seat. Everything had been drained from him in a race that had seemed to last a lifetime. Yet only two minutes had passed.

He heard the pandemonium that was taking place in the stands, and then the announcer said, "Ladies and gentlemen, the winner will be announced as soon as the photograph has been developed. A few seconds, please." After a pause he added, "Will Mr. Ramsay and Mr. Bauder please keep their colts on the track?"

Alec didn't need to await a picture of the finish to know who had won this second heat of the Hambletonian. It had been Bonfire by the nose of his red-hooded head.

Revolt!

17

Alec wasn't consciously aware of much that happened during the next few minutes. He heard the beginning of the announcement that Bonfire had won but little else. His ears were deaf to the bedlam of the crowd as he drove Bonfire up the stretch, wanting only to get his colt back to the paddock.

The announcer said, "Introducing the winner of the second heat of the Hambletonian, Bonfire, a son of the Black out of Volo Queen. Owned by Mr. Jimmy Creech of Coronet, Pennsylvania, and driven by Alec Ramsay."

At the track gate and all along the roped aisle leading to the paddock were hundreds of people with their hands outstretched, trying to touch the sweated colt. The police kept them back. And then Henry was there at Bonfire's head. Alec saw him. Henry had taken over. Everything was all right now.

Once they entered the paddock enclosure the shouting multitude was left behind. But in its place were the reporters and photographers.

Angrily Henry pushed his way through them, his free hand clenched as he waved it in the faces of those closest to him. "Get back! Give this colt air!" he kept saying.

He halted Bonfire in front of his stall and told Alec to leave. Then once more he hurled a fiery outburst at the group. "Move away, I tell you! He needs more air. Go on now! The race ain't over yet."

The press grudgingly stepped back from Bonfire but Henry wasn't satisfied. "Move more!" he yelled, waving his arms wildly, his face distorted both with anger and with concern for Bonfire. "Where's that paddock judge now? Where is he? Somebody keep these people away!"

Shutters clicked as pictures were taken. Bonfire jumped and Henry held him close. The uproar finally brought paddock officials to Henry's aid and they moved the group farther back from Bonfire.

Henry had stripped the colt of his harness when Jimmy Creech came running up to him, wanting to help. Henry shoved him toward the barrage of reporters and photographers. "Best thing you can do for your colt," he said, "is to tell those people what they want to know so they'll clear out of here. If Bonfire don't get more air an' some quiet there won't be another heat in him."

A look of concern came to Jimmy's eyes at Henry's words. He nodded and walked toward the group, straightening his scrawny shoulders as he moved along. He had bred and raised this colt, winner of a Hambletonian heat. That much was *his*. No one could ever take that from him.

Jimmy remained with the group for many minutes, telling the newsmen all they wanted to know . . . yet realizing, as they did, that little of what he said would be used unless

Bonfire won the Hambletonian. Lively Man and Ringo had been subjected to the same kind of thing after winning the first heat.

Later he watched them go, and then returned to Bonfire and Henry.

"Thanks for gettin' rid of them," Henry said.

"It was a pleasure," Jimmy answered, smiling and picking up a sponge. "—a real pleasure."

Alec watched Jimmy at work, the sponge moving easily, almost caressingly, over Bonfire's back. He couldn't remember ever having seen Jimmy smile before.

Unable to sit still any longer, he got up and began cleaning the harness and bridle. Henry told him to take it easy and rest but he continued working. It was impossible to take it easy now. How many minutes to go before the next heat? Not too many.

The light cooler was put over Bonfire.

"I'll walk him," Jimmy said.

"No, I'll do it," Henry returned adamantly.

Jimmy went to Alec. "Let me clean the harness then," he said. "I got to be doin' something. Sit down, Alec. Rest. You'll be racing."

Reluctantly Alec let him take the harness. Everybody was telling *him* to sit down, yet *they* had to keep themselves busy. Didn't they understand he felt just as they did?

"You timed your bid perfect, Alec," Jimmy said. "Y'caught old Si Bauder by surprise and got the jump on him. Never seen better drivin'."

Alec thought, *Don't give me any credit for good timing, Jimmy. If that black filly had hung on a second more, I would have lost the race for our colt.*

But he kept quiet. He didn't want to talk. He wanted to be let alone.

"Now we got the pole position," Jimmy said. "Short way around for us this time, Alec!"

The short mile close to the rail. But only if he got Bonfire out in front and kept him there. Could he do it? Would Bonfire last another mile, even a short mile? At Roosevelt Raceway Henry had said Bonfire couldn't go three Hambletonian miles. Had Henry changed his mind? Did they have a chance in this third heat? Bonfire was blowing hard but so were the other colts.

Alec left Jimmy's side while the little old man continued talking. He went to Henry and Bonfire, noticing for the first time that Bear Cat too was being walked between heats. Falling in beside Henry, he said, "I guess Bauder's changed his ways a little."

"It looks like it," Henry answered. "Maybe I shouldn't have said anything to him today." He paused. Then, "I wish you'd sit down and rest, Alec. You're blowin' as hard as the colt."

Alec tried to smile. "That's just why I need walking too," he said. "It's been months since I raced, and never in anything as tough as this. This is a long grind, Henry."

"I know," Henry answered. "You and the colt could have used more work for it." He turned to Alec, his eyes losing their hard professional concern and a softness creeping into his voice. "But your head's in good shape. You gave him a smart drive, Alec. You did everything right at the right time. No one could have done it better."

"No one could have had a better colt," Alec said.

"I know that too," Henry returned.

They stopped before the water pail and Bonfire shoved his

head eagerly toward it. Alec offered the water to him, count-
ing the colt's swallows and finally taking the pail away.
"That's enough for now," he told Bonfire. And then to
Henry, "Let me take him, please."

Henry let go of the halter and lead shank but moved with
Alec up the row. Many seconds passed before Alec finally
asked Henry what he really wanted to know.

"Will he go another heat?"

"Sure," Henry said lightly, "and so will you."

"But fast enough? I'm serious, Henry. I want to know."

"I can't tell you, Alec. I really don't know the answer."
Henry paused, and Alec didn't look at him. "I *think* he's
strong enough to beat most of them," Henry added.

"Most of them?"

"Well, all but one then," Henry answered. "I'm worried
about that colt over there, Alec. An' the guy who's drivin'
him."

Alec looked at Bear Cat. The brown colt was walking easily. He didn't seem to be breathing as hard as Bonfire. But
what Henry had said was nothing new or startling to Alec.
He'd known all along that Bear Cat and Si Bauder loomed
larger than anyone else in their path to a Hambletonian victory. But Bonfire had beaten them once. He could do it
again.

"Bear Cat," Henry said, "is the only colt here, includin'
ours, who's been trained right and aimed right for this race.
That's my opinion, anyway. He's been brought along slowly
and beautifully over a long period of time. He's at his peak
today. He's got a world of speed, an' stamina as well."

Henry stopped talking, his eyes following Bauder who
went to Bear Cat to feel beneath the cooler.

"He's got a smart old trainer too, a guy with a lot of common sense. Bauder warmed Bear Cat up lightly, and had him ready for the race. Si wasn't worrying none about the first heat. It was the second and third heats he knew he could take."

"But he didn't," Alec said. "—not the second."

"No. You surprised him, all right. But that man isn't as sore as you might think he is. He only figures you've delayed him a little. Now he'll have to take the third and *fourth* heats."

"You mean we'll have to go still another mile heat if Bear Cat should win this one?"

"Sure," Henry said. "How else you goin' to determine the winner of the Hambletonian? But the whole field wouldn't go a fourth heat. Just the three separate heat winners—Lively Man, Bonfire and Bear Cat."

Alec smiled grimly. "Don't rush things, Henry. He hasn't won the third heat yet."

"No, an' don't you and Bonfire let him. If it ever came to a fourth heat, Bear Cat would be the only one in the race. Bonfire wouldn't have much left, and Lively Man would have less."

They continued walking Bonfire but said nothing more. The colt's hoofs beat off the minutes, and then the seconds. Finally they knew their waiting was about to end. Bonfire was put in his stall. Jimmy stayed with them, but he too was painfully quiet. Only Bonfire made any noise. He jerked the tie ropes, trying to get at an occasional fly that bothered him.

For Henry it was the worst time of all. The necessary work that had kept him busy was done. In addition to these final minutes of waiting, shared by Alec and Jimmy and everyone else in the paddock, he had to decide how best to fix the eyecup so it could *not* be used again.

Henry glanced at Alec, who was standing near Bonfire's head trying to give the colt relief from the flies by waving his hand. Alec had forgotten *or* had forgiven him for what he'd tried to do before the second heat. Henry couldn't decide which it was. But it didn't matter. When the call came and Bonfire was hitched to the sulky, Alec would remember to check the cord and cup. Henry was certain of that. But he'd find a way. He'd been given one last chance, and it was all he needed. No slip this time. No backfire.

Henry wished Jimmy would go away. What he had to do was difficult enough without having Jimmy around as a constant reminder of what this third and perhaps final heat of the Hambletonian meant to him.

Henry turned away. And it meant just as much to him and Alec. They wanted to see this son of the Black win the Hambletonian. He had every right to win. Never had a Hambletonian been raced as fast as that second heat. And Bonfire had courageously come from behind to win it!

What about the third? Would it be as fast? Perhaps faster? Henry was certain that the thousands of people at Good Time Park were asking themselves the same questions. They knew as well as he did that this next heat would be strictly a two-colt race. Lively Man was licked. He wouldn't be able to stand the fast pace. Only Bonfire had a chance of beating Bear Cat, but no one, including Henry, knew how much of a chance. It would depend on race strategy, on the breaks of the game.

On one side of the stall hung the red hood. Henry looked at it a long while. It had worked so well in the second heat.

How often had Alec opened and closed the eyecup during that race? Many, many times. And now it was going to be taken away from Alec and Bonfire.

Henry took his eyes off the hood. He *had* to do it. He was playing for high stakes, higher than any this famed Hambletonian could offer. And he was counting on a courage and self-confidence Alec and Bonfire didn't know they possessed *because the hood kept them from knowing.*

Finally the call came. "Hook 'em up, boys. We're going out in a few minutes!"

Everyone in the paddock was glad the call had come. The Hambletonian colts were harnessed. The last time that day for almost all of them. Only Bear Cat could make a fourth heat necessary for himself and Lively Man and Bonfire. Few of the other drivers expected to beat Silas Bauder's brown colt. It was up to Bonfire or Lively Man to end the Hambletonian with the coming heat.

Alec was the first to reach for the red hood, and he said, "You help Jimmy, Henry. I'll take care of this end."

The old trainer knew then that Alec had *forgiven* him rather than forgotten. Alec wasn't going to leave the colt's head until they had stepped onto the track. Realizing this, Henry accepted his *only* alternative. His jaw became set and the skin drew tight about his cheekbones. He went to Bonfire's head and removed the hood after Alec had slipped it on.

Alec reached for it. "What are you doing? That was on right, Henry."

"I'm not goin' to let you put it on him, Alec," Henry said quietly.

"Okay, put it on yourself then," Alec answered. "But

hurry up. We have no time to kid around."

"I'm not kiddin'. I'm not puttin' it on him. No one is."

It was only then that Alec realized what Henry meant. His face grew a shade paler and then he said again, "Put it on him, Henry."

Jimmy moved closer to them, wide-eyed in his surprise. "What are you two arguin' about?" he asked. "The colt's ready to go. Come on now. They're waitin' for us."

Neither Alec nor Henry paid any attention to Jimmy. Silently they stood looking at each other. Henry's face was whiter than Alec's and deep lines cut into his heavy jowls.

"I had this hood made," he said. "I paid for it myself. It's mine, and now I'm takin' it away. I'm takin' it because Bonfire doesn't need it any more . . . or *you* either." He turned away and walked down the paddock row, his strides coming fast but his shoulders slumped like those of an old, old man.

Alec stood still, but Jimmy made use of his legs. He ran after Henry, catching him at the paddock gate. Henry pushed Jimmy away from him, and then was lost in the great crowd.

Jimmy returned to the stall and stood beside Alec, his thin lips moving a long while before the words came. *"Why? Why now?"* he kept repeating.

Alec knew why, but there was no point in telling Jimmy now.

The paddock judge called, "Hurry up your colt, Ramsay! You're holding us up!"

Alec put on the bridle. "Come on, Bonfire," he said. "We're going out. We're going clean."

"All the Way Home . . ."

18

The announcer said, "The horses will now go behind the gate for the third heat of the Hambletonian."

They passed the stands in the final two-column parade with introductions and warm-up scores over. They were in their post positions earned as a result of the previous heat. Bonfire led the parade, the first horse in the first tier. Directly behind him came Bear Cat.

Alec's eyes left Bonfire only for the track marshal riding before them. Beyond the marshal at the top of the stretch awaited the mobile gate. Alec paid no attention to the nine colts following him or to the eight others across the track. But he knew they were there, that all eighteen would be going behind the gate to race as hard as they'd done in the two previous heats. He didn't take for granted, as did almost everyone else, that this time it would be strictly a two-colt race. He assumed nothing in so large a field where anything could happen to change the complexion of a race. He hoped only to get Bonfire out in front, giving him a chance to race as he'd done before.

Alec looked at Bonfire's clean head, bare of anything but the light, open bridle. His colt did not turn to the left or the right. He kept his eyes straight ahead, his ears pricked, watching the gate come closer and closer. He knew very well what was about to happen. He was ready and eager. He didn't seem to miss his red hood.

Alec wasn't furious with Henry any longer. Whatever anger had been in him had left the moment he had seen Henry merge with the crowd, taking the hood with him. There was no getting it back, no turning back. It was too late for anger. All that was left was to accept what Henry had said: *"I'm takin' it because Bonfire doesn't need it any more. . . ."*

Alec hoped desperately that Henry was right. "I mustn't even say I *hope* he's right," he told himself. "I must *know* he's right." Never before had he doubted Henry's judgment. Why doubt it now, when so much depended on the outcome of this heat?

They passed the mobile gate with its barrier wings folded and clear of the track. A short distance farther on the marshal waved his riding crop, signaling their release. Alec turned Bonfire, as did the drivers of the other colts in the first tier.

It wouldn't take long to find out if Bonfire needed the trick hood. Racing room would be close moving behind the gate. Any second Alec would know the answer.

Over the public-address system the announcer said, "The horses are now in the hands of the starter, and are moving behind the gate."

The stands quieted as the wheels of the limousine began turning and the colts in the first tier followed the barrier wings. Behind them came eight other colts.

"Bring up your colt, Bauder!" the starter ordered. "You're lagging."

Alec had Bonfire close to the moving gate without touching it. The rail to his left seemed to stream by, going faster and faster as their speed increased. The position on Bonfire's right was open as Bear Cat strode behind the others in the first tier, his brown body alongside Alec.

It was just like the start of the second heat, Alec thought. Silas Bauder would bring Bear Cat up with a rush, attempting to have his colt going at top speed when the gate opened.

But this time the starter was insistent. "Come up, Bauder, or we won't go off!"

Bear Cat began inching toward the barrier wings, his head now at Bonfire's hindquarters.

Alec glanced past the brown colt to Lively Man in the third post position. Ringo had his colt's nose touching the barrier, ready to get away fast, determined to make up for having lost the rail to Bauder in the previous heat.

Bonfire was steady. He kept his eyes straight ahead while Bear Cat came up closer and closer on his right. Instinctively Alec moved the small finger of his right hand. But no cord was tied there. There was no eyecup to be closed.

The beat of hoofs mounted. The crowd was on its feet, no longer shouting with shrill voices but hushed in expectation of what they were about to witness. Faster and faster the field moved down the stretch until hoofs and engine rose in a mighty crescendo.

In that ever-mounting rush to the starting line Alec kept his eyes on his colt, watching for the slightest movement that would indicate Bonfire's fear of Bear Cat. But his colt saw nothing but the speeding gate before him, and his demands to be turned loose became stronger and more insistent.

Alec's small finger moved again, and this time he realized what he was doing. He closed his finger over the line to keep it still. He wanted no reminder. And yet he felt his tension mounting. He kept his eyes on Bonfire's head and ears. There still was no sign that Bonfire had any fear of Bear Cat, now racing alongside stride for stride a little behind the gate. Certainly Bonfire knew of Bear Cat's presence but it wasn't bothering him. If Alec needed any other assurance that Henry had been right, it was in his hands. He felt Bonfire's determination to get out in front of those racing beside him, his tremendous *will to win*.

The lines were wet from Alec's perspiring hands. He glanced at Bear Cat. He found himself moving his little finger again. Hot, salty perspiration stung his eyes. He was anxious, worried—for himself or for Bonfire? The leather in his hands was slipping and he dug his fingernails into it to hold it fast.

Bonfire shook his head at the tight rein. *Too tight,* Alec knew. He'd drawn back on the lines. What had caused him to do that? Bear Cat had his nose ahead of Bonfire. Alec told himself to loosen up, to give his colt a little more line. Nothing was wrong. Bonfire was going well. They had the pole position. The best position. A short mile for Bonfire, and at the end of it the famed Hambletonian.

A few more strides to go to the starting line. Bonfire shook his head again, angry now. They were dropping back too far! As Alec tried to loosen his hold on the lines, he found that his hands were trembling.

His colt was steady but he wasn't. Had he been depending upon the hood more than Bonfire? Was that what Henry had meant all the time? *"I'm takin' it because Bonfire doesn't need it any more."* But there'd been something else. Hadn't Henry added, *". . . or you either"*?

That was it! Alec's heart pounded hard as a rush of anger swept over him—anger at *himself* for what he was doing to his colt! He let the leather slide through his fingers, giving Bonfire full line.

The colt's release came a fraction of a second too late. The barrier wings were no longer in front of the large field. Bear Cat was more than a stride ahead of Bonfire, and Lively Man was a half-length beyond Bear Cat, with Ringo rushing him as he'd never done before!

Alec raised his hands, urging Bonfire on, but he was sickened by the handicap he'd forced upon his colt. He knew the effort it would take not to lose the rail to Lively Man and Bear Cat. Already Ringo was starting to move his roan colt in front of Bear Cat. He was using his whip, getting every possible bit of speed from Lively Man.

Alec felt cooler, calmer. He had to think fast now. There was no time for anything else. It was what he needed.

He lowered his hands, slowing Bonfire from that desperate early drive he'd begun. He knew he couldn't prevent Bear Cat from taking the rail from them. But it would still be a short mile for Bonfire. He wasn't worried about Lively Man, and he'd send Bonfire after Bear Cat going down the backstretch.

Approaching the first turn he saw Ringo cut sharply in front of Bear Cat. Bauder slowed his colt to avoid an accident, enabling Bonfire to move up on Bear Cat. Alec saw the anger in the old driver's eyes at Ringo's careless and dangerous move.

Now Lively Man was in front and on the rail with Bear Cat just behind and to his right. Alec began moving Bonfire off the rail. He didn't want to be pocketed there in back of Ringo. Soon Lively Man would tire. Bear Cat was moving alongside him even now, sweeping into the turn. Lively Man was slowing sooner than Alec had expected. The roan colt's strides were becoming very heavy and sluggish.

Alec glanced back at the field coming up on his right. He had time to move all the way out from the rail and go past Lively Man with Bear Cat. He gave Bonfire more line, drawing him wider on the turn, and then began moving up just behind and to the right of Bear Cat.

He saw Ringo glance at Bauder as Bear Cat raced by, and then the young raceway driver went for his whip again. For a second the roan colt stayed with Bear Cat under Ringo's tireless urging. But then Lively Man had no more left to give.

Alec was closer to Ringo than anyone else when it happened. Lively Man stumbled and regained his stride, only to stumble again. Alec slowed Bonfire, realizing what was coming. *Then Lively Man went down!*

Ringo's arms swung wildly as he tried to keep himself from being thrown from the sulky, but there was nothing for him to grab hold of. He was pitched forward, striking the track on one side of his colt and rolling away from him.

Alec had pulled Bonfire to the right, and now he pulled him harder at the sight of Fred Ringo sprawled on the track before them. Everything he did came instinctively. He caught a fleeting glimpse of Ringo's face as it was turned toward him, and then he waited for the heavy thud of Bonfire's hoofs on flesh. But miraculously Bonfire managed to avoid the driver.

Only when it was over did Alec's mind begin to function again. Above everything else he could remember what Ringo's face looked like—a murky gray in color, not unlike the face of another whom he *hadn't* avoided. He shook his head to rid himself of that horrible mental picture. Where did he have Bonfire? There was the press of horses all around him.

The announcer's voice came over the loudspeakers. "The field passed Fred Ringo without injuring him or his colt," he assured the crowd in a calm voice. "Now at the quarter-mile it's Bear Cat in front by two lengths. Princess Guy is second. Mismatch is third. Lord Bobbie is fourth. The rest of the field is bunched. King Midas is on the rail and just ahead of High Noon. Bonfire has dropped back after having run out to avoid the accident. He's in the middle of the field."

Now Alec was able to see the colts racing on either side of him and in front, all so close, leaving no room to get Bonfire clear of them. He could only wait and hope for something to break after they came off the turn. No short mile for Bonfire now. Nothing but a grueling, tortuous road that might never be opened to them. Dead end? Was that it?

No, he had to find a way out for his colt! Then why wasn't he looking for it? Why was he holding Bonfire back, just waiting and hoping for the breaks to come their way? Why wasn't he making his own openings?

The grouped field came off the turn and entered the backstretch. There was no change in positions, still no room for

Bonfire to get clear. Far ahead raced Bear Cat followed by Princess Guy, Mismatch and Lord Bobbie. Were they to be the only ones contesting Bear Cat's right to win this race?

Tangiers was directly ahead of Bonfire, and to that colt's right were Star Queen and four others spread across the track. Star Queen had come off the turn a little wide and didn't move any closer to Tangiers going down the backstretch.

Alec saw the opening there but disregarded it. He wasn't going to risk hurting Bonfire in an attempt to go through such a narrow hole. He wasn't afraid, he told himself. He was just being cautious for the sake of his colt. It was much smarter to stay behind, to *wait*.

He gave Bonfire no command but the colt suddenly shifted stride, pushing his head into the small opening. Alec realized it was too late to stop him. Bonfire already had his body between the sulky wheels on either side of him. Alec measured the distance with his eyes, and then decided there was just enough room for his sulky. He gave Bonfire more line and they squeezed between Tangiers and Star Queen. But once more the road was blocked. Alec slowed Bonfire to keep him from running into Silver Knight, who was now in front of them.

Bonfire's will to win had so far got them only a length closer to the front of the packed field. And Bear Cat was drawing farther away. Yet Alec had responded quickly to Bonfire's gameness, to his refusal to wait. He felt some of his colt's courage sweep back to him, driving away all caution, all thought of Tom and Ringo or anything but the race to be won.

No more waiting. One move at a time, one length at a time

brings us closer and closer to where we want to be!

Still wanting Bonfire to go as short a mile as possible, Alec looked at the colts racing between him and the rail. No chance to make a move there. No room at all. On the outside, there was an opening between Cricket and Victory Boy. But how would he get Bonfire over there with Star Queen in his way?

Alec glanced at the big chestnut filly just off to his right. He waited a second more before making his move, and then edged Bonfire over. Slowly, ever so slowly, he forced Star Queen out with him. One stride at a time he moved Bonfire over to the opening between Cricket and Victory Boy—and then he went through!

Again there were colts in front of them, but Bonfire was on his way. "One move at a time," Alec kept telling his colt, "one move at a time!" And then he took Bonfire over on the inside, this time between Chief Express and Big Venture.

Drivers shouted at him angrily, but he kept moving Bonfire more and more to the front until only King Midas and High Noon were between him and the leaders in the distance. To pass them he had to take Bonfire outside again. He'd given up all hope of a short mile for his colt. All he asked was a chance to race! Alec bore out again, and this time Big Venture and Bonfire drew alongside High Noon and King Midas. For a second the four colts raced stride for stride, and then the blood bay colt went to the front.

Alec and Bonfire had reached their goal! Only empty track was between them and the leaders. Bonfire went forward eagerly as they swept into the second turn.

The call came over the loudspeakers, "At the half-mile, Bear Cat has increased his lead over Princess Guy by four lengths. Lord Bobbie is next. Mismatch has dropped back to fourth. And then comes the rest of the field. Bonfire is on the rail and in front. He's followed by King Midas, High Noon and Big Venture. Cricket is . . ."

Alec had Bonfire where he wanted him, and going around the turn he slowed his colt. Bonfire fought but Alec refused to give him more line. The colt needed a rest. They'd gone a half-mile the most difficult way. Repeated short bursts of speed were more demanding on a colt than a sustained drive. He kept Bonfire close to the rail, ignoring the field behind him and refusing to look at the colts ahead. "Let's rest now," he told Bonfire. "Take it while we can get it. It won't be for long."

He heard the hoofs behind him coming a little closer but he wasn't worried. Neither King Midas, Big Venture nor any of the other colts had the speed left to catch up with Bonfire or the leaders.

They entered the long back straightaway that led to the final turn. But to Alec nothing mattered now but a "breather" for his colt. He'd learn all he wanted to know within a very few seconds.

He was about to ask a lot of Bonfire, perhaps too much after what his colt had been through. He would give him free line all the way to the finish. The time had come. They couldn't wait any longer. He released Bonfire. *Now it was all the way home or nothing!*

As the blood bay colt sprang forward, Alec looked ahead. Mismatch was the closest to them and losing ground before Bonfire's mounting speed. He was off the rail and Alec decided quickly *not* to go around him.

Mismatch was a beaten colt, his strides coming fast but

getting him nowhere. Bonfire reached him sooner than Alec had expected. He had his colt moving into the opening between Mismatch and the rail before he realized how small the opening was. For a second he tensed as Bonfire's hoofs narrowly missed the other sulky wheels. Then the blood bay colt went through with wheels turning hub to hub. Bonfire went to the front, bearing down on Princess Guy and Lord Bobbie who raced in Bear Cat's wake.

Silas Bauder and his brown colt were moving into the last turn. Their lead over the others hadn't been lengthened going down the back straightaway, but Bauder was content. Bear Cat was comparatively fresh and ready to go an all-out drive to the wire. It had been a short mile, an easy mile for the brown son of Phonograph.

Alec already had Bonfire in his final drive. Would his colt last? Bonfire was gaining on Princess Guy and Lord Bobbie. The turn was just ahead. Alec didn't want to take Bonfire wide around it. He wanted to save every foot of ground he could for his colt. Princess Guy was on the rail with Lord Bobbie matching her stride for stride.

Alec moved Bonfire a little away from the rail approaching the turn. Yet he kept an eye on Princess Guy, knowing that sometimes she was inclined to swing a little wide going around turns. If it happened this time she'd take Lord Bobbie out with her, and perhaps leave an opening on the rail for him and Bonfire to go through! Neither of the drivers ahead seemed aware that Bonfire was so close. But soon they'd know.

Alec brought Bonfire out a little more from the rail, ready to go around the two drivers if necessary. He'd save time and distance if the opening came on the rail. The timing was important. There could be no hesitation, no weighing one advantage against another. Bonfire's strides were smooth, and coming faster and faster. He must do nothing to cause them to falter in the slightest—not if they were to catch up with Bear Cat!

Princess Guy wobbled a little. Alec drove Bonfire back toward the rail as the black filly *swung wide,* taking Lord Bobbie with her. Bonfire was heading toward the hole that opened up more and more as Princess Guy left the rail. There was no turning back now. Alec had made his decision.

The announcer called, "At three-quarters of a mile it's Bear Cat still in front by four lengths. Princess Guy and Lord Bobbie are racing together. Bonfire is moving up strong *on the inside!*"

Alec kept his eyes on the opening ahead, unaware that Silas Bauder had looked back and, seeing Bonfire so close, had begun his final drive for the finish wire.

The opening was now large enough for them to go through and Alec called to Bonfire, although there was no need to urge this colt to greater speed. His hoofs barely touched the track before they were off again. He was only a few strides from the opening when his way was suddenly barred.

Under hard, strong hands Princess Guy had been stopped from going wide and was being taken back to the rail. She sprinted as the whip was used, and the opening was closed to Bonfire!

Alec had no time to think, his move came instinctively. He slowed Bonfire, pulling him to the right and away from the sulky in front of him. Princess Guy's driver glanced back, surprised to find Bonfire so close and then frightened as the colt's head swung over him. He braced himself for the accident that never came.

Alec saw the opening left by Princess Guy's return to the rail. Lord Bobbie was still going wide and a little behind the black filly. It was as small a hole as anything they'd gone through during the race, and it was becoming smaller as Lord Bobbie moved off the turn into the homestretch. Alec would have hesitated if he could, but there was no other place for him and Bonfire to go!

Bonfire pushed his head between the straining, spinning wheels of the two sulkies, reaching for the front, for the open clay before him.

Alec watched the opening close about his colt. He shouted at Lord Bobbie's driver, demanding racing room. He knew that if he didn't get it there might be a terrible accident and he and his colt might never be able to race again. He kept shouting to the other driver to move over as Bonfire raced ahead in his courageous drive.

The opening held as Bonfire thrust his body through, and Lord Bobbie's driver realized then how near they were to having an accident. He didn't close the hole any further, but he didn't pull away, either.

Alec knew his colt was getting through, and for a fraction of a second he cast his eyes at the gleaming hubs of the two sulkies that were now scraping against each other. Then he wrenched his gaze from them and looked ahead at the brown colt who was racing alone at the top of the homestretch.

A second passed and then the terrible suspense and waiting were over. Bonfire was out in front, the sulky clear! Five lengths ahead was Bear Cat. Bauder's hands were raised as his colt went faster and faster toward the finish wire. He was confident nothing would come up from behind to surprise him this time!

There was no need for Alec to urge Bonfire on to greater speed. Bonfire saw the lone colt ahead of him and that was enough. Perhaps, too, he heard the voices of the crowd and knew where he was and how much distance he had still to cover.

Alec realized that he had nothing more to do, that his work was done. There were no dangers in the stretch beyond, there was no strategy necessary. He had only to sit as close to his colt as possible, furnishing no obstruction to the wind that whipped on either side of Bonfire. Nothing but speed mattered now, and his colt was giving all he possessed without any prompting from his driver.

To Alec's right passed an ever-increasing blur of faces, so he knew they were sweeping by the bleachers. There were less than two hundred yards to go. The roar of the grandstand descended upon him. Tiers upon tiers of seats cast their deep shadows on the track. The sun had been left behind. Perhaps only a hundred yards to go now.

Alec wanted desperately to look ahead but would not, could not bring himself to move from behind Bonfire. He kept himself as small as possible and as *one* with his colt. He listened only to the powerful swish of the great muscles in front of him and watched only the flashing of silver-shod hoofs beneath his seat.

Suddenly, without having to move his head, he saw what he had been waiting to see. On Bonfire's left appeared the green-and-yellow silks of Silas Bauder. The old man's whip hand was raised, his wrist moving in furious rhythm as he demanded more and more speed from Bear Cat. But still the green-and-yellow silks kept falling back.

Then Alec was able to see Bear Cat! Bonfire had his head at the brown colt's hindquarters. Alec tried to blink the stinging sweat out of his eyes so that he might see better. Bonfire was catching up with Bear Cat and yet Alec felt no great elation. For above the brown colt's head rose the judges' stand. Too few yards away! Bonfire's gallant, courageous sprint had begun a fraction of a second too late. A black filly had beaten them on that final turn.

Suddenly Alec felt the seat beneath him move as though it were jet-powered. It was jerked and catapulted forward. Alec would have sworn both sulky wheels were off the ground. But he had no time to think any more of this. The lines were alive in his hands, almost pulling him out of his seat. He shoved his feet hard into the stirrups to keep his balance as the green-and-yellow silks, a brown colt, and the judges' stand all merged into one. He knew the race had ended, but he did not know its outcome.

"... And That's the Way It Should End"

19

All those who witnessed the blood bay colt's amazing sprint down the homestretch described it as nothing compared to what happened only a few yards from the finish wire. They said Bonfire seemed to gather himself in a great effort without loss of stride or time. They compared it to a tightly coiled spring that is suddenly unwound. They admitted his hoofs must have touched the track but said it was hard to believe because he went forward at such incredible speed. Those on the rail had something to say about the wheels of the sulky as well. They claimed the forward thrust of the blood bay colt carried the wheels and Alec Ramsay off the ground. Actually he was in the air, they said, going past Silas Bauder. They never expected to see another Hambletonian like it, and certainly none as fast. Bonfire's new record would stand a long, long time.

There was no order to the crowd when Bonfire came back up the stretch, protected by a line of policemen. People jumped the track rail and tried to reach him. In front of the judges' stand the police formed a circle around the colt and his driver.

The announcer said, "The photograph has been developed and the winner is Bonfire." But no one listened. The photograph simply made official what the crowd had known for several minutes. They pressed closer to the winner's circle, those far in back jumping up and down in an attempt to see over those in front.

Alec was kept in the sulky seat by track officials. There were so many people in the circle, and all were strangers. Cameras clicked away, and he became more and more concerned for Bonfire's safety. A man he'd never seen before was holding his colt while the pictures were being taken. Microphones were held in front of him, and he had to say something about how happy he was to have driven the winner of the Hambletonian. . . .

Alec brushed the sweat from his face. Where were Jimmy and Tom and George? He couldn't stand any more of this *alone*. It looked as though the presentation ceremony would go on a long while. More and more people were entering the winner's circle, shaking his hand, stroking the colt.

Then he heard the announcer say, "Will Mr. Jimmy Creech please come here. Mr. Creech of Coronet, Pennsylvania."

But the request was needless. The announcer hadn't finished before the circle opened to admit Bonfire's owner. Jimmy helped Tom while George cleared the way, demanding that the crowd stand back from the boy. The three waved and grinned at Alec, but went to Bonfire. Jimmy had the colt's worn red-and-white blanket, and he put it over Bonfire despite the protests of the photographers.

Alec knew everything was all right now . . . except that Henry was not there. Where was he? Wasn't he coming into the winner's circle at all? He must be somewhere around, watching all this.

The announcer said, "And now, ladies and gentlemen, introducing the Hambletonian winner Bonfire, sired by the Black and out of Volo Queen. Mr. Jimmy Creech, his breeder and owner, will now accept the Hambletonian Cup. . . ."

Television cameras were on Jimmy and microphones were shoved before his thin mouth. The crews told him to smile and he had no trouble complying with their requests. It was the day Jimmy had long awaited. Proudly he stood beside his colt.

Tom's hand was on Alec's shoulder and Alec asked him if he'd seen Henry. Tom shook his head. He was too moved by all that was taking place to speak. He looked at Bonfire and Jimmy as though he wanted to impress the scene on his mind forever.

George stood at Bonfire's head. Alec looked past him and beyond the swarm of faces in the winner's circle. His searching gaze swept over the great stands. Never would he be able to locate Henry among all those thousands of people! Tom left him to stand beside Jimmy at the request of the photographers.

It was then that Alec saw the tiny patch of crimson in the lower grandstand. He studied that particular section more closely, and then slowly he unbuttoned his racing jacket, slipping it off without attracting his friends' attention. He folded it and left it on the sulky seat, together with the red-and-white cap.

Then he went to the uncrowded side of Bonfire, where he would be inconspicuous, and touched the colt proudly, lovingly.

At the height of the presentation ceremonies, few people paid any attention to the slim boy in the T-shirt who left the ring. He climbed the track rail and merged into the crowded stands. He didn't stop until he had reached that small patch of crimson.

"How come you're keeping this, Henry?" he asked, taking the hood from his friend's hand.

"Just a memento," Henry answered, his eyes on the track ceremonies. "—my souvenir of the Hambletonian."

"I'm sorry, Henry," Alec said.

"Nothin' to be sorry about. I never seen a more exciting race."

"I mean I'm sorry that I didn't listen to you before."

"It's not listenin' to me that wins races," Henry answered. "You drove to win, that's what counts. An' you had a colt with heart and courage, just like his old man."

He rose from his seat, his arm encircling Alec's waist. "Let's get packed, kid," he said. "Our work's done."

They turned toward the winner's circle again. Over the loudspeakers came Jimmy's nasal voice, praising his colt and all those who had made the Hambletonian victory possible. Henry shrugged his shoulders disinterestedly when he heard his own name mentioned. Alec said, "Cut it out, Henry. You know you're just as thrilled as the rest of us."

"I'm too old to be thrilled any more," Henry answered. But there was a look in his eyes that belied his words. "It's *their* party," he added. "C'mon."

Alec hesitated a moment before following Henry through

the crowd. His eyes remained on Bonfire while Tom, George and Jimmy stood close to the blood bay colt, their hands upon him. Finally Alec turned away. Henry was right. All this belonged to them and he might as well leave now. He'd see Bonfire again, back at the farm in Coronet, where the colt would be taken. For Jimmy, Tom and George there was only one horse, Bonfire. But he and Henry had other sons and daughters of the Black to care for and to race—*even the Black himself!*

Just before Alec caught up with Henry the announcer requested the presence of "Mr. Dailey in the circle, please." Henry hesitated a second but then went on.

"I take it you're not going back," Alec said.

"Nope," Henry answered. "Leave 'em alone with Bonfire. That's the way it started an' that's the way it should end."

Alec nodded in agreement; together they left the great stands.

ABOUT THE AUTHOR

Walter Farley's love for horses began when he was a small boy living in Syracuse, New York, and continued as he grew up in New York City, where his family moved. Unlike most city children, he was able to fulfill this love through an uncle who was a professional horseman. Young Walter spent much of his time with this uncle, learning about the different kinds of horse training and the people associated with each.

Walter Farley began to write his first book, *The Black Stallion,* while he was a student at Brooklyn's Erasmus Hall High School and Mercersburg Academy in Pennsylvania. He finished it and had it published while he was still an undergraduate at Columbia University.

The appearance of *The Black Stallion* brought such an enthusiastic response from young readers that Mr. Farley went on to write more stories about the Black, and about other horses as well. He now has twenty-five books to his credit, including his first dog story, *The Great Dane Thor,* and his story of America's greatest thoroughbred, *Man O' War.* His books have been enormously successful in this country, and have also been published in fourteen foreign countries.

When not traveling, Walter Farley and his wife, Rosemary, divide their time between a farm in Pennsylvania and a beach house in Florida.